Charlie Marlowe, Bigfoot Investigator

Don Shearer

Published by Don Shearer

All rights reserved. Except for use in a review, the reproduction or utilization of this work in whole or in part in any form by any electronic, mechanical or other means, now known or hereafter invented in some ludicrously sideways future, or in any information storage or retrieval system that reeks of cranky skunk apes, is forbidden without the written permission of the publisher.

While all of the bigfoot encounters portrayed in this volume are loosely based on actual, well-documented events, this is a work of fiction. Names, characters, locations, incidents, dialogue, food types, beverages, unsupervised quadrupeds and bipeds, hedgehog holograms and sarcastic slugs are either the product of the author's imagination or are used fictitiously, and any resemblance to actual persons, living or dead (or mostly-dead), events or locales is not only entirely coincidental, but staggeringly pointless.

As usual, no humongous, hairy, huge-footed primates were harmed during the composition of this work. However, a bigfoot brouhaha did flummox the stomachs of a herd of homely hominids.

CHARLIE MARLOWE, BIGFOOT INVESTIGATOR

PRINTED IN THE UNITED STATES OF AMERICA

Copyright © 2021 Don Shearer

Cover design copyright © 2021 Brian Cundle

ISBN: 979-8-74-531012-6

The Other, Other Page

Other books by Don Shearer (available on Amazon.com):
- Bigfoot Bedtime Stories: Tall Tales for All Ages
- From the Deep Forest

Other works (music albums) by Don Shearer, available on Amazon.com, YouTube and other lofty, sonic e-places:
- Strange Terrain
- Across the Dry Plains: New Mexico Portraits in Sound
- Strange Orbit
- Socially Inept (sorry, this one's out of print)
- Monster in the Sitting Room (sorry, this one's *WAY* out of print, although still quite relevant...)

Musical monster by Barbara Shearer

Foreword

The process of circumnavigating the continental U.S. in an RV isn't necessarily glamorous, particularly when you're pursuing gigantic creatures known to be quite stinky, weird, and downright uncooperative. However, I hope you'll go along on this rollicking rumble of a run with our resident bigfoot investigator, Charlie Marlowe, and his beagle pup Betty. Along the way they run into all kinds of things that they struggle and strain to comprehend. Plus, they eat and drink too much. So if you're interested in frightening monster encounters, digestive atrocities and subsequent guttural expulsions (brap!), please join the journey with Charlie Marlowe, Bigfoot Investigator.

Contents

Acknowledgments

1	Charlie and Betty Set Out	1
2	Sasquatch in the Pumpkin Patch	16
3	Lone Star Snake Sling	32
4	Old Stumpy Strikes Again	46
5	Juvies and Jalopies	60
6	Full of Hard Knocks	79
7	Swamp Squatch of the Allegheny	98
8	A Sasquatch Uncorked at Salt Fork	116
9	Pawnee Pony Peril	128
10	Close Call at the Camper	147
11	A Michigan Monster Makes its Way	165
12	Just Spooling Around	188
13	Fear in the Four Corners	212
14	There's No Place Like…	234

Acknowledgments

To **Barbara Shearer**, thanks for all the continuous inspiration, collaboration and editorial contributions to this work. *Charlie Marlowe, Bigfoot Investigator* has truly been a joyous team effort—a team of two. Sharing this wacky ride with you, Barb, is something I'm grateful for every day.

To **Casey Shearer**, thanks for reviewing, commenting, cogitating and commiserating about this work. I appreciate all of your creative ideas and your sharp eye for detail. Plus, the pooch portrait you provided conveys copious canine comedy.

To **Brian Cundle**, thanks for the mesmerizing cover art that fully captures the spirit of massive monsters and those valiant field researchers (whether hound or human) who pursue them.

To **Sybilla Irwin**, thanks for the enchanting, fully fear-inducing bigfoot witness sketches appearing in chapters 1, 3, 5, 7, 8, 11, 12 and 13 of this book. Your supportive work—on behalf of these creatures and the astonished humans who occasionally witness them—is always valuable and appreciated.

Additional photo credits...

...include LINE.17QQ.com, LegendOfBoggyCreek.com, Pinterest.com, Oklahoma State Parks, CryptoVille, VRBO.com, Lake O' The Pines, Free Campsites, Mickey's Place, Sasquatch Canada, ThinkStock, eBay, U.S. Fish and Wildlife Service, VisitNC.com, Carolina Mountain Vacations, OrthoCarolina, Carolina Forestry, LakeTillery.com, Forest Fire BBQ, Pixabay, Allegheny National Forest Visitors Bureau, Salt Fork State Park, Hickory Point Campground, AllTrails, Lake Superior Spirit, San Diego Zoo, BrewGoat, The Spruce Eats, Playful Goose Campground, RV Trader, Nomadic Lifestyle Magazine, Bigfoot Encounters, Snapwire, wtsenates.com, Good Free Photos, Out There Colorado, BigfootCasts.com, Casey Shearer, Don Shearer, Worldwide Elevation Map Finder, Wiki-Pet, Crate & Barrel.

1

Charlie And Betty Set Out

As darkness fell, Charlie Marlowe balanced what remained of his margarita on the low stucco backyard wall as he stood and looked pensively out over the City Different, otherwise known as Santa Fe, New Mexico. Charlie enjoyed the typical nighttime fragrances of this city—a mix of diverse aromas from countless busy eateries in the area, with a hint of soothing piñon fireplace smoke wafting through the dry air at day's end.

Resting at Charlie's feet on this early summer night was his trusted beagle pal, Betty. She was a tricolor "pocket" beagle, somewhat smaller than the more common 15-inch beagle variety. Charlie and Betty were essentially inseparable, as the dog accompanied Charlie on virtually every outing he took. Lying down next to where Charlie stood, Betty had fully mastered the distinct pleasures of canine inertia. She was flopped over and snoring in the flower garden mulch.

Charlie had recently retired from his job teaching English and composition at a community college in Santa Fe. Now he devoted most of his time to adapting to the pace of "civilian" life—free of early classes, late classes, faculty meetings and budget brouhahas.

A quite pudgy man with white hair, a matching beard and wire-rimmed glasses, Charlie could have doubled as a Santa Claus figure if educational work hadn't otherwise engaged him professionally.

Francesca Marlowe, Charlie's brunette native-New-Mexican wife of more than 30 years, stepped out the back door to check on Charlie and Betty.

"What are you two shady characters up to now?" she asked as she approached the two collaborators in evening indolence.

"Well dear, we're just mutually enjoying the close of yet another darkening diurnal cycle," answered Charlie, with his characteristically articulate style. (For fun, he often wielded his abiding flair for the syntax and rhythm of the English language. His very intelligent wife often did the same.)

Francesca regarded Charlie's margarita glass and queried him about its seeming emptiness. "Was your drink up to snuff?" she asked, "or do we need to dial 911 for an emergency tequila intervention?"

Charlie giggled lovingly at his wife's fanciful inquiry.

"In fact, young lady, I was just preparing to hoof it back into the domicile for a refill," said Charlie. Betty perked up as the two humans headed back to the house. She followed them in through the sliding glass door.

Their home was a one-story, light brown pueblo-style home nestled in a comfortable neighborhood amidst the low rolling hills and abundant scrub piñons typical of this part of the desert Southwest. Here, the stucco-enrobed homes were not very close together and there were none of the curbs and gutters germane to more suburbanized regions. The neighborhood had the true New Mexico feel of wilderness running right up to residences.

Throughout Charlie and Francesca's home was beautiful lighting (with many fixtures ensconced in nichos), bountiful wood viga and latilla trim, a tongue-in-groove ceiling in the great room, and a big kiva fireplace as a central focal point of that room.

Now seated comfortably inside on a rivet-bordered leather couch and loveseat (with Betty in Charlie's lap), Francesca and Charlie partook of some deeper discussion amidst the candlelight.

Sitting next to Charlie and holding a glass of dark pinot noir, Francesca asked him, "Well, my venerable citizen of the world, it looks to me like you're pretty well caught up on your rest. It's August now. What exactly are you going to do now that you've escaped the cruel confines of academia?"

Charlie laughed a bit and tugged at his beard—a natural gesture when one is preparing to grapple with a weighty subject.

He eventually said, "I'll have you know that I've got a perfectly comprehensive plan on what I'll be doing over the long term. I believe I'll share it with you in several months—once the core concepts have coalesced."

Quickly grasping Charlie's wordy though feeble effort at fudging, Francesca tilted her head to the side and said with mock disdain, "Charles, I suspect that your 'perfectly comprehensive plan' is about as sturdy as a dry leaf on a windy day."

"Now, you know I'm quite fond of observing dry leaves as they scuttle about the premises and the sidewalks," Charlie replied. "Often I suspect those dry leaves may have more of a directional orientation than do I, and they always seem to get where they're going...so let's not unduly denigrate them."

Francesca shook her head at Charlie's less-than logical leap into leaf-dom.

"I don't know what I'm going to do with you, sir," she said to Charlie finally. "It doesn't take much to inspire you to leap over the garden wall of logic and into the whimsical world of... whatever."

Charlie laughed some more, grabbed his margarita glass, and reached over toward Francesca for a conciliatory clink of glasses.

"As soon as I truly know what the plan is, honey, you'll be the first to know," he said to Francesca. Then, however, he looked downward into his lap at his dog Betty, and revised his statement.

"Okay, you'll be the *second* to know," he said enthusiastically.

Francesca bit her lip in mock disapproval and said, "You are absolutely incorrigible, dear Mister Marlowe."

The couple soon wrapped up their quiet celebration of the evening and turned in for the night.

The next day, Charlie puttered around the residence working on small fixup projects and considering next steps for himself. Betty was rather fully engaged in tearing a donkey dog toy to pieces and scattering the shredded detritus around the house.

Unlike Charlie, the slightly younger Francesca had not retired and was still actively employed as an admissions staffer at the community college where Charlie had worked. So, on this day, she was already at work, leaving man and dog to fend for themselves.

As he made his rounds attending to various domestic chores, Charlie let his mind wander toward one of his primary interests with which he'd like to re-engage: tracking reports of bigfoot/sasquatch encounters.

Charlie was an active member of the Sasquatch Sighting Documentation Database, otherwise known as SSDD. This was an all-volunteer group dedicated to collecting sighting reports from people around North America and beyond, including Canada. The technical hub of the operation was a website where citizens could complete and submit an online form documenting what they've witnessed or heard, the geographic region and climactic conditions at the time, and the number of witnesses involved.

Captured in the database, the reports would be evaluated by volunteer administrators who, in most cases, would assign the reports to one of the widely geographically scattered SSDD members who would follow up with the witnesses by phone, eliciting and gathering whatever subsequent detail they could glean from those who had come in contact with the creature(s).

Charlie was one of those SSDD members who volunteered his time occasionally to follow up on reports. His interest in bigfoot was quite longstanding, and he shared this interest with like-minded friends and colleagues around the country. However, given the great diversity of the staff at the community college and the concomitant impressionability of young students, Charlie hadn't considered it wise to share his monster involvement with others at the college, risking misunderstanding and/or ridicule.

Now that he was retired, however, the self-censoring shackles had loosened. Charlie was feeling freer to consider getting more active in the pursuit of bigfoot reports. When notified, for example, by Jimmy Spencer, one of the primary website administrators at the SSDD, Charlie now let his mind travel to the locations and situations that citizens had reported.

As retirement time was proceeding apace and Charlie continued to dedicate time and energy to guiding sasquatch witnesses through processing their deeply unsettling experiences, the sighting accounts now seemed to tug at him a bit more than previously. He began to wonder if there was more he could do in fully documenting the experiences of those who had seen something truly unexplainable.

On this day, it was an afternoon mental brainstorming session where Charlie's thoughts on the monster issue began to crystallize a bit more.

With thoughts and potentialities swirling, Charlie sat down in the comfy loveseat with Betty to relax and watch one of the seminal sasquatch movies of the 20th century: "The Legend of Boggy Creek." This was a near-documentary about a series of scary bigfoot sightings near Fouke, Arkansas back in the late 1960s and early 1970s. Some of the monster imagery in this film was quite compelling, although none of the actors in the film likely took home Academy Awards for their portrayal of relatively hapless, terrified citizens. It was a fun video ride, however, for modern day viewers interested in the emergence of bigfoot lore.

Francesca got home from work in the very late afternoon. Charlie had begun warming up some leftover green chilé pork stew and tortillas, so the house smelled wonderful upon

Francesca's return, and dinner wouldn't be too far off. However, looking at the TV screen, Francesca immediately grasped what Charlie and Betty were doing.

"Really?" she said to Charlie. "Boggy Creek again?"

Charlie hesitated for some time, alternately scratching his chin and the back of his head.

"I'll acknowledge that this one's a little clunky, and the music is slightly baffling, but it has some importance in the sasquatch oeuvre," he explained in reply.

"How many of these oddball oeuvres did you watch today?"

"This is the only one, dear," Charlie reassured. "However, I also patched up the leaking drip line out back, changed some light bulbs, and repositioned the toilet flapper ball in the side bathroom," he said with an official summary-type tone. "We're flushing with the best of 'em now, don't you know."

"Well, I guess the day wasn't a *total* loss," said Francesca.

Through the glass back door, Betty had spotted an overstuffed mourning dove on a nearby tree, and she dutifully woofed the puffy gray fowl flapper.

In the middle of a luxuriously steamy, spicy, comforting green chilé-infused dinner, with Betty sitting attentively at Charlie's feet awaiting any potential hot dropsies, Charlie contributed a sudden and resounding proclamation.

"You know, Francesca," he began, "I'm going to head out and investigate these things." He offered no further explanation.

"What 'things' would these be, my bewildering yet apparently resolute mate?" Francesca asked eloquently.

"I'm talking about sasquatch, of course," replied Charlie. His demeanor became more serious and insistent now, with words delivered at a faster pace. "As you know, I've been helping follow up on reports by phone for a number of years now. *Every* once in a while, one of the SSDD staff is fortunate enough to live in proximity to a recent sighting, and they can travel to the site and conduct witness interviews in person, take evidence measurements, and snap photos. Chained to the 8-to-5 grind for the last 237.5 years," he continued with expansive exaggeration, "I've had no opportunity to conduct one of the valuable in-person investigations of the sightings. I think that needs to change now," he concluded.

"So you're going to roam the wilds of the United States in search of sasquatch accounts that can be documented on behalf of a deeply disbelieving populace?" Francesca asked. "Where will you go?"

Charlie again scratched his head and his bearded chin.

"Well, I believe I'll let the reports guide me," he replied finally. "I'll put together a draft itinerary based on recent reports, and travel to the encounter locations for my follow-up. There could be quite some distance to them."

"That sounds like a pretty far-flung expedition; how will you travel?" asked Francesca.

Charlie resumed his recurring head and chin scratching. He thought back to the many road trip vacations he had taken with his wife and pooch in the family's old medium-sized Ford recreational vehicle. Traveling in the RV, the trio had gone on extensive excursions all throughout the Four Corners region of the Southwest, and sometimes beyond. Perhaps he could simply drive further this time...a lot further.

"Why, I'll roll with Motor Myrtle!" Charlie said in a sprightly manner, referring to the RV that the couple had given a name, currently parked next to the house at the rear of the driveway. "She's a bit underutilized right now and could use a good long outing."

Francesca thought about that for a moment, including the potential risks to her husband that could be involved.

"So you're just going to drive out of here all alone?" she asked, not really expecting a positive reply.

"Well of course I won't do that, honey," Charlie said with a twist of his head. Francesca warmed a bit at the apparent nod to her indispensability.

"Betty will be with me every step of the way, won't you girl?!" Charlie said jovially to the dog, who was at this time sound asleep in a comfy dog bed across the room.

"Oh, so I get it," began Francesca. "You're going to run off with the pretty young thing and leave me behind to slave and worry." Francesca was implicitly referring to her full-time duties at the college and the unlikelihood of getting extensive time off for a long road trip. The trip would mostly likely be purely a man-and-mutt expedition.

"It'll be fine," reassured Charlie, with an air of deeply unwarranted overconfidence. "Betty will have my back."

Francesca turned and looked directly at the dog sleeping in oblivious comfort, and then back at Charlie.

"That dog wouldn't have your back if a herd of mini goats was biting your butt."

"Hmmph!" exclaimed Charlie indignantly, yet lightly. "Some people!"

This denouement, although maintaining loving undertones, ended the discussion for the day. It would resume at another time quite soon.

Over cold drinks out back the next day, late in the sunny afternoon, Francesca set out to query Charlie about some of the potentially inconvenient details of near-solo travel out on the open road.

"Do you have adequate funds tucked somewhere to finance your middling mystery tour?" she asked with Beatlesque notes.

As usual, Charlie needed a few moments to formulate a solid reply.

"I do have a couple of healthy accounts tied to my credit cards, and that should be plenty for subsidizing a national tour," he said with an expanding measure of boldness. "Unless," he continued spontaneously, "I get shaken down by the infamous Bandit Bigfoot of Middle America." With this ludicrous reference, Charlie's impish, self-satisfied smile expanded.

"Okay, what about Myrtle?" Francesca asked, returning to practical realms.

"What about the old dear, old dear?" Charlie replied quickly.

"Hey now, don't refer to me as an 'old dear' in the context of a ramshackle recreational vehicle," Francesca admonished tartly.

"Well, I'd say she's in pretty good shape," said Charlie, rapidly redirecting. "I'll probably run her into the camping center for a maintenance checkup just to be sure," he added. He'd done this several times previously, with favorable mechanical results and a tad more confidence upon hitting the road.

"Well, I imagine that's a good idea," was Francesca's reply. "What types of places will you touch down in?"

Fortunately, Charlie had already begun formulating this part of his travel plans. "I'm already piecing together a rough list of fairly recent sightings that I can plan on investigating," he said. "I'll also be flexible on selecting destinations if new reports come in from the SSDD while I'm out on the road. I fully expect this to happen. So, I'll make advance plans at some RV campgrounds near encounter locations where I know I'll be working (particularly those that require prior reservations and payment), plus I'll hit campgrounds and those big box retailer parking lots that certainly don't require reservations," said Charlie in conclusion.

"How about food this time?" asked Francesca.

"Well," began Charlie thoughtfully, "I'll stock up on food for the RV freezer at the outset and on the road, plus there's some tiny chance that I'll stop in at a pub or two along the way for some local eats and brews...just to sample the regional cuisine," he said.

"A pub or two, on that long trip?" retorted Francesca. "I'm guessing you might hit a pub or two *before you've even gotten out of town here*," she added with no uncertain emphasis.

"Now now, dear," responded Charlie quickly and defensively. "This will be no 'moveable feast,' and there will be no excess of mobile carousing on the itinerary."

Francesca hesitated a moment before saying, "Well, I'll check up on you by phone periodically to see if you've gotten thrown in the slammer for having gotten hammered."

"The nerve of some rhymers," said Charlie gruffly but with a smile.

He got up and walked inside, ostensibly to use the facilities, but more likely to refill his swill.

Francesca and the dog were not too far behind him in entering the house. Francesca soon resumed her queries, in the kitchen this time.

"Do you plan to meet up with anyone you know out there?" she asked.

"Well, I'm not yet sure what order the investigations will take in terms of geography, but two SSDD-affiliated people I've communicated with so far about possible joint investigations are Sarah Whitson in Texas and Emmi Flowers here in New Mexico," Charlie explained.

"No male collaborators out there?" Francesca asked with perhaps an extra spike of curiosity.

"Up to this point, I've only texted or phoned with the other SSDD gents," said Charlie, "but as the newer reports come in, that could certainly change."

Francesca held his gaze upon this response, and Charlie soon got the message.

"Of course there's no romantic interest in my life other than you, sweetie," said Charlie to his wife quite dramatically. "You're the love of my life, and the only other girl who's ever caught my eye that way has four legs and is a snoring lump of fur in the corner," he said, clearly referring to Betty.

Charlie originally obtained the dog from a rescue shelter when she was about six months of age. She had previously lived a pretty perilous life on the street, but now was spoiled rotten with love and gustatory comforts.

"Have you noticed Betty's kind of extra gassy lately?" Francesca asked.

Charlie laughed. "I'd say were all a bit manners-challenged these days."

Over the next several days, Charlie went about the practical tasks of getting ready for the colossal schlep across the country in the RV. At local retailers, he stocked up on items such as dog kibble and treats, frozen dinners, bread and lunchmeat, bottled water, cereal, other breakfast foods, plaster of paris for potential track casting, and, perhaps, a bit of booze. (He sometimes pined for the epicurean comforts of home when he was stopped overnight in any location.)

With Francesca's help, Charlie also ran Motor Myrtle to a Santa Fe RV facility that sold new RVs and did maintenance work on existing rigs. Before work at the college one day, Francesca paralleled Charlie on a drive-along to the shop. They dropped off the RV and Francesca drove Charlie home. With any luck they'd be able to pick up the rig at the close of business that day without excessive expense.

At home, Charlie packed up his clothes, bedding and investigative gear for eventual loading into the RV.

While busied with the packing process (during which Betty slept upside down in a comfy recliner), Charlie occasionally checked his SSDD link via his laptop. Doing so, he noticed that he'd received a fresh SSDD report that had come in from Oklahoma.

Charlie immediately contacted Jimmy at the SSDD to inquire whether the Oklahoma case still required follow-up investigation. Jimmy quickly responded in the affirmative, welcoming any help that Charlie could provide.

On the phone, Charlie said to Jimmy, "I'll be out in Oklahoma in a couple of days, I believe."

And with that, Charlie applied himself to outlining his proposed investigative route across the nation—beginning with the fresh report in OK country. He checked his national atlas, which was opened upon the office desk, against all the recent reports that had come into the SSDD, whether the cases had been followed up on or not.

Charlie then began to plot an informal, drafty travel loop beginning in the Southwest and heading east through the Gulf states to Florida, well up the into East Coast, over to Ohio and up into states in the Midwest. Then the planned route would take the travelers back down into the Southwest, to the expedition's conclusion. At least, that was the plan.

And just like that, the outset of the quixotic quest had been triggered.

With Motor Myrtle back in the home stable and ready to roll, Charlie and Francesca talked into the evening about any and all remaining details of the trip that could be identified at this early juncture.

Francesca helped Charlie pack up the RV. Portable luxuries for both man and dog were checked and double checked, then stowed efficiently for travel.

The couple spent one last night cuddling and giggling at the panoply of unknowable vicissitudes they'd encountered in their joint lives over the years, and they said their goodbyes.

The next morning, after a luxurious pancake breakfast (with Betty devouring a generous shard of bacon), the two travelers took their positions in the RV. Of course, Charlie was driving, and Betty took the front passenger seat in the "shotgun" position.

"Call me when you get in," said Francesca, referring to the initial Atoka County, Oklahoma destination, as Charlie smiled at her, pulled out of the driveway and embarked upon the first big investigative trip of his life.

Off they rolled toward southeastern Oklahoma, nearly ten hours and more than 600 highway miles away.

From Santa Fe they headed south to the "Big I" interchange in busy Albuquerque, then picked up I-40 heading east through the Tijeras Canyon and out onto the plains. Crossing northern Texas (through Amarillo), the major highway I-40 took them east toward Oklahoma City, where the travelers stopped for a welcome break from the innumerable potholes dotting some stretches of highway in this region. Then they headed south to Atoka County.

Their first brush with monsters awaited them.

2

SASQUATCH IN THE PUMPKIN PATCH

Charlie piloted Motor Myrtle well into southeastern Oklahoma, where he arrived feeling rather bushed after the lengthy drive. He realized that he was a bit out of shape when it came to long road treks. Oklahoma was only a state away from New Mexico, but once out on the open highways, passing countless farm fields, ranches and rest areas, one realizes what a big country the U.S. is and how long it can take to traverse it on the ground.

The individual who reported a bigfoot sighting to the SSDD was Norman Hess, an older man who had witnessed a creature on his property in Atoka, Oklahoma. Atoka was a mostly rural setting, with houses spread well apart, many farms, and a small city center. The local population was barely 3,000 people.

The area was known for the presence of the Boggy Depot Monster, a large, hair-covered creature apparently seen along the riverbanks and creeks in and around Atoka over many years.

Charlie drove directly to the address of Mr. Hess that he had gotten from Jimmy at the SSDD. The home was located well off the main road at the end of a long gravel driveway, and was situated among quite a few tall, leafy trees. The Hess home was a tan-to-brown multipart structure featuring a two-story A-frame main living quarters and a closed breezeway connecting to a two-car garage. At the front of the A-frame portion of the building was a high raised porch or deck bordered by light-colored wood slat deck railings, with sizeable trees just to the right and left of the deck.

On this warm August afternoon, Mr. Hess was sitting on the front porch in the shade with his dog as Motor Myrtle drove up.

As they rolled to a stop, Charlie said to Betty, "Well girl, you may have thought I was steering us into utter oblivion, but here we are!"

Betty jumped down off the passenger seat in anticipation of being let out for an apparent social call. Followed closely by Betty, Charlie stepped out of the RV and vigorously stretched his arms, legs and lower back after the lengthy drive. He looked at the front of the house and saw a seated man smoking a pipe and observing him.

"Are you Mr. Hess?" he shouted toward the house.

There was no immediate response. "Yeah, that's right. Who wants to know?" the man eventually asked in a slightly grumpy, wary tone, likely inspired by his having observed a strange recreational vehicle drive all the way up his long driveway to the house.

"Why it's me, Charlie Marlowe, Mr. Hess!" intoned Charlie enthusiastically.

"Oh yeah, the bigfoot guy," said Norman. "I wasn't really sure when you were going to show up," he added.

"I'm terribly sorry, Mr. Hess, I thought Jimmy would tell you it might take us several days to get here," explained Charlie.

"Well, I guess I don't rightly remember, now that I think about it" admitted Mr. Hess. Apparently warming a bit, he said, "And you can call me Norman. My wife does that when she's not using a cussword," he added drolly.

"Well, that's just fabulous," said Charlie as he stepped up onto the deck and reached out to shake Norman's hand. Norman wore glasses, had buzz-cut gray hair, wore an old pair of work pants with matching shirt, and perpetually clutched his pipe. This was clearly a convocation of codgers.

Betty was right behind Charlie on leash, and she took great excitement in spotting Norman's dog, an elderly-looking yellow Labrador retriever. Tails wagged with excitement, and the dogs traded posterior sniffs in order to obtain the requisite full measure of each other.

Observing the canine conference, Norman said, "This here's Annie. She's had lots of adventures around the property over the years but she doesn't do so much now…kind of like me," Norman added.

"Well *hello* there, Annie," said Charlie with great gusto as he leaned down to rub the dog under the chin. "It's indeed an honor to make your acquaintance," he added with his typical verbal grandiosity.

"Have a seat, Charlie" offered Norman. "Um, can I get you an iced tea or something?" he asked somewhat thoughtfully.

"Oh, that would be *more* than marvelous," replied Charlie as he plunked down on one of the cushioned deck chairs.

"Well then, I'll be right back…unless I get bushwhacked in there," said Norman, referencing the ostensible perils of spousal relations.

Charlie giggled robustly.

"Well, this is a comfortable spot, isn't it then, Betty?" asked Charlie of his four-footed friend, who was scuttling about the deck with Annie. Charlie stretched again and sat back to relax a bit more in the soft chair beneath the pleasant trees.

A couple of minutes later, Norman returned with a tall glass of iced tea. Charlie immediately brightened and sat up at the sight.

Norman said, "I had to give some blood in order to get this, so I hope you enjoy it, Charlie."

Charlie again giggled in gender solidarity.

Norman took a chair across from Charlie, and Annie immediately walked over and curled up at his feet. This looked like a familiar repose for the gold-to-white-colored dog and her retired owner.

Charlie reached into his bag and extracted his laptop, which he set on his lap, opened and fired up for notetaking purposes.

"Do you spend much time out front here?" asked Charlie of Norman.

"Oh yeah. Annie and I ponder the universe for many hours a day out here. The shade's pretty good around here even if the indoor company is sort of subpar."

Charlie was again amused at Norman's take on his marital muddles.

"So...why don't you describe for me what you witnessed here, Norman," suggested Charlie.

Norman took a few long drags on his pipe, leaned back and looked off into the sky for nearly a minute.

"This was something I'd never believed in or ever thought I'd see around here," began Norman. "I'd heard about the Boggy Depot Monster or Boggy River Monster—whatever you want to call it—but a local legend is one thing, and a huge five- or six-hundred-pound visitor on your property is another," concluded Norman with substantial closing emphasis.

In line with the "boggy" references, Norman's home was located in an area near the Muddy Boggy Creek in Atoka.

As Norman continued to recount his sighting, Charlie typed and interjected occasional clarifying questions.

Apparently, Norman had been sitting on this very porch with Annie at dusk one night several weeks before. He was almost done reading the paper that day, as the outdoor light was fading, when he heard some unsettling growling utterances from the direction of his mostly dirt pumpkin patch at the edge of his yard, which abutted a heavily forested area.

Suddenly, several good-sized deer crashed through the woods on that side of the house, from the general direction of the pumpkin patch. Norman considered this development extremely unusual. What had caused it?

The deer streaked in near lockstep across the front yard of the house, directly in front of Norman, moving in Norman's sight from right to left. Looking rather panicked, the animals quickly jumped over a fence at the far left edge of the property and ran up a hill at the back of the adjoining property. All of this hasty locomotion took only several seconds.

Soon Norman heard more crashing in the woods (this time quite noisier than the deer), after which a gigantic dark figure appeared to Norman's right. The figure looked extremely tall and heavy. It strode powerfully out of the pumpkin patch area and entered the residential part of Norman's property, which was grass covered and neat. This creature was shaped like a man and walked on two legs, but was covered in hair and was much, much larger than a human.

It took just a few seconds for the creature to cover the entire width of the property, right in front of Norman, even though the creature was not running.

The creature seemed to take no notice of the human and the canine on the front porch. It appeared wholly focused on its pursuit of the deer.

As the creature got to the left edge of the property where the deer had bounded over the fence, it smoothly reached up and stepped over the fence with a single stride, and followed up the hill after the deer.

Thinking about it later, Norman estimated that the top of the fence was at least four feet off the ground, so if the creature so easily stepped over it, the being must have been somewhere in the vicinity of eight feet in height...perhaps more.

Also, considering the obvious bulk of the hairy creature, Norman estimated that it would have been at the very least 500 pounds in weight. A weight of 600 pounds or more wouldn't have been at all out of the question.

Given the fully hair-covered nature of the striding beast, along with its tremendous height and obvious weight, Norman was stunned at what he'd witnessed as the events of the evening started to sink in.

What apparently amused Norman was that despite the presence of a disquieting racket and a massive, imposing creature, Annie the dog didn't budge or bark during the entire episode. Norman wasn't sure how that was possible, but it may have been that the dog's comfort superseded any interest in adventure.

In Norman's continuing account, he said that upon exiting the property and scaling the hill, the bigfoot made a few more extremely unsettling grunts or calls, and was soon gone in the woods surrounding his closest neighbor's house...which was not terribly close.

After the creature had left the scene, Norman apparently sat still in his chair for several minutes, highly amazed that he had seen such an astounding display of mammalian behavior. He had almost certainly witnessed—up close—the regional monstrous creature of legend, right in his front yard.

Charlie had stopped typing notes and was listening with rapt attention as Norman finished his sighting account.

"Well, that's just remarkable, Mr. Hess," said Charlie to Norman with an extensive measure of respect and gratitude. He followed up with several clarifying questions.

"At the time of this sighting, did you detect any odor emanating from the creature?" he asked.

The man thought about the question for a moment, dragging on his pipe, and replied, "No, there wasn't any smell that I noticed. The creature went by so quickly that maybe there wasn't any opportunity to drop the proverbial sasquatch stench," he said, grasping what Charlie was likely after via his query.

"Did you spot any footprints or other lasting evidence of the creature's presence?" asked Charlie.

Norman again considered the question.

"As a matter of fact, there were some large footprints that I noticed over in the patch," said Norman, pointing with his pipe to his right, toward the pumpkin patch. "I can show you that if you'd like."

"Yes, of course," said Charlie, "I'd like to mosey about the property a bit if it's okay with you."

"I don't see why not," replied Norman.

Charlie grabbed his backpack containing his investigative tools. The foursome (two bipeds and two quadrupeds) initially walked over toward the fence at the left edge of the property. Betty (on leash) led Charlie while Annie (running loose) was on her own.

As they approached the fence, Charlie asked Norman, "Can you show me where the creature went over the fence?"

Norman walked up to the yard border and grabbed the top of the wire fence with one hand.

"This is right where the creature grabbed the fence, pushed it down just a little and stepped over it," he said to Charlie. "You can see that it's still a little bent down here," pointing to a slightly twisted horizontal wire segment at the top of the fence.

Charlie reached down for his camera and trusty tape measure. He took a picture of the top wire of the fence where it was bent. Then, holding the tape measure case between his shoes, he unspooled the tape from the ground up to measure the height of the fence.

"Fifty inches, or just a little less," Charlie announced to the group. "And you say the creature stepped right over this?" he asked Norman to possibly elicit some clarification.

"Yes, with one hand pushing down on the fence slightly, the creature stepped one leg after the other right over the fence and started bulldozing up that hill really fast," said Norman, pointing to the rear portion of the neighbor's yard.

Charlie stood still and looked in the direction the sasquatch had walked. "And you estimate our fence hopper was in excess of 500 pounds?" he asked in an attempt to get whatever additional detail might be available.

"Yeah, well, I was in the military a long time ago, then worked as a deputy for a number of years, so I'm pretty well accustomed to observing and sizing up perps," said Norman with a slight chuckle.

"Some outsized perp *this* must have been," echoed Charlie, still looking up at the neighbor's hill.

"Biggest damned thing I ever saw," commented Norman.

Changing tacks, Charlie said, "Well, it's starting to darken up a bit, so why don't we head over to the patch prints?"

"That'd be fine with me, Charlie."

The group again trundled across the yard, this time in the opposite direction, toward the dirt pumpkin patch and adjacent tree line. Charlie extracted a flashlight from his backpack.

Norman bent over a bit in an attempt to spot any extant footprint marks. Charlie did the same, although he didn't know exactly where to look.

"Here's one," announced Norman. "It's really big, although not too clear."

Charlie hurried over to where Norman was standing and looking down. Shining a flashlight on the bare footprint, Charlie could see that the impression was quite a bit larger than a human's print, although the toe detail seemed to have gotten smudged somewhat in the intervening weeks.

Setting the flashlight down, Charlie again reached for his tape measure and stretched it out next to the footprint.

"Just over seventeen inches," said Charlie to the others.

"Man, that clod was one big hopper," exclaimed Norman.

Charlie left the tape measure locked in place, then reached for his camera that was currently attached to a strap around his neck. Although the light was fading, Charlie was able to get a couple of fairly clear shots of the footprint and accompanying tape measure, utilizing the camera's flash.

Charlie and Norman continued walking around within the pumpkin patch, looking for additional prints.

"Here's another one," said Norman.

Again, Charlie scurried over to take a look. This print was not as deep in the soil as the first print, and it had less outline detail.

"It's not as clear as the other one," explained Charlie, "but it's still valuable." He took several photos of the second print the men had discovered, next to the 17-inch tape measure segment.

This pattern repeated itself as Charlie and Norman gradually approached the tree line from whence both the deer and the monster had emanated. Charlie took a few more photos of deep footfall impressions (though not many with good detail), then the men started heading back toward the house.

They had walked about 50 feet when Betty and Annie almost simultaneously started growling. Both dogs were looking toward the far end of the pumpkin patch near some trees and heavy brush. Norman grabbed Annie by the collar, and Charlie held tightly to Betty's leash as she strained it to its limits. Both men began feeling queasy and disoriented as from some unseen force.

As everyone tensely looked in the same direction, a low growl erupted from behind the tree line. It started quietly at an incredibly deep pitch then rose very quickly in pitch and force, lasting five or six seconds altogether. Norman later said the sound reminded him of a bear growl only deeper, more focused, and probably angrier. He believed the sound was the most terrifying noise he had ever heard, and it made his skin crawl with discomfort.

The low blast of sound impacted both men and dogs as would a shock wave. The creature's infrasound expulsion essentially froze all four figures in place, overwhelming them with instantaneous shock and fear.

Charlie and Norman both took the sonic attack as an unequivocal warning from the creature for the group to stay away.

As each individual tried to regain his or her senses and figure out what to do next, Charlie spotted someone standing partially obscured by a large tree at the far edge of the melon field.

He said quietly to Norman, "Uh, our fence-hopping perp is here, I think."

Norman strained his eyes in the gloaming as he looked across the lot, saying, "My God, look at that!"

The creature's shoulders and head bowed out at an angle from behind the tree as it observed the men. It was performing a partial-body peek. The head appeared to be seven or more feet up the trunk of the tree. Norman thought the creature's face looked ape-like yet somewhat human at the same time, though the head was larger than a human's and pointier at the back of the skull. There was ample beard and cheek hair visible.

At the sight of the huge creature, Betty suddenly began rapid-fire barking with total abandon. Given this new canine cacophony, the creature stepped fully back behind the tree.

Within seconds of disappearing, the creature let loose with another rumbling roar, this time of greater volume and urgency than the first vocalization. At the end of the growl, the creature emitted almost a gruff, barking-type coda. This tree-obscured individual clearly did not want to be perturbed by pumpkin patch personages or pooches.

Again, the humans and dogs were dumbstruck with shock after the creature's vocal blast. The bigfoot was claiming this territory for the evening, and no one would have any capacity to object.

"Uh, back to the house now, guys," said Norman with a quivering yet insistent voice. He didn't wait to gain consensus on his suggestion of a hasty retreat.

Turning and bending down a bit, he held onto Annie's collar and scampered straight back to the deck and front door of his house. "G'dang, I'm too old for this," he said as he trudged clumsily toward the house, still bent over holding the dog, amidst a heap of his own aches and pains.

Charlie was right behind Norman lugging his backpack and holding onto Betty for dear life. His camera bounced off his chest as he rapidly crossed the grass.

All four group members quickly climbed the stairs of the deck and reached the front door of the house. Just before entering, Charlie stopped and turned around.

"You know, I would very much like to have gotten a better look at that creature," he said somewhat ruefully, "but I don't believe he was in general favor of our presence."

Charlie issued this unquestionable understatement and then ducked inside to join the others. Norman quickly closed and locked the door behind Charlie, turning on the outside lights to discourage potential uninvited night visitors.

Norman invited Charlie to sit down and rest at the kitchen table. Norman's wife Pamela, a slight woman with short gray hair, wearing dark slacks and an oversized t-shirt, was working on a fried chicken dish that Charlie and Betty both found quite enthralling.

"What was all that racket you men were making out there?" she asked Norman while starting to heat up some corn on the stove.

"Well, I guess you might say that Mr. Boggy River paid us a call," said Norman in reply to his wife.

"Mr. Boggy River? Who on earth is that, your collection agent?" Pamela asked.

"Oh shoot, it's that old legend of a big, hairy creature that's been seen around here over the years."

"You mean he was *here*?" asked Pamela, incredulously, nearly dropping an empty pan on the floor.

"Yup, we just saw him about five minutes ago. Plus we *heard* him, and maybe you did too. *Man*, did we hear him."

Pamela stood still, clearly trying to process the encounter information.

"I did hear a scream or roar of some kind," she said, "but I didn't know what it was." She waited a moment, then said, "I thought maybe you'd scared one of your ugly girlfriends."

"We're quite certain it was the aforementioned sasquatch," interjected Charlie, "right at the edge of the melon patch and willing to growl us out of the place."

Looking down at the floor toward the exhausted quadrupeds, Norman said, "These dang dogs nearly got right up on him, and *man*, he didn't take to that!"

"Oh my goodness," said Pamela in reply. "You probably coulda' fed the dogs to him and he would have left you alone."

At this gleefully insensitive comment from his wife, Norman emitted a slight growl of his own.

Everyone was then still and silent for a few moments around the table. The only sounds were the bubbling corn and the soon-to-be-snoring dogs settling down in the hallway.

Over the fried chicken dinner late in the evening, the human trio discussed some of their experiences with bigfoot creatures.

Charlie explained his informal role in the SSDD, and Norman recounted some of the local tales of the Boggy River or Boggy Depot Monster.

Charlie listened with rapt attention, of course, even taking some notes on his laptop, but eventually it was time for him to call it a night and transport his canine companion to their place of rest for the evening.

So, Charlie, Pamela and Norman said their goodbyes, and Norman accompanied Charlie and Betty on their short walk out to the RV.

As Charlie ushered Betty up the steps into Motor Myrtle, Norman said to him, "Hey, do you think that dang thing's still around here?" Norman was clearly referring to the gigantic fence jumper and irritated vocal acrobat.

"He may well be," replied Charlie, "but he'll almost certainly move on overnight. None of these creatures stays put for very long. You probably want to keep Annie inside tonight, though," he added as a cautionary note. Charlie's closing assessment provided at least a bit of reassurance to Norman, whose interest in having an eight-foot-tall cranky monster again in his yard was less than substantial.

Once rolling, the travelers made their way into town to stop overnight in a parking lot at an Atoka Walmart store, on South Mississippi Avenue.

Later, working at the laptop, Charlie finished documenting what he gathered today at the Hess residence, including downloading some photos from his camera to the laptop.

Charlie considered this an excellent start to the trip, given that he and Betty had an actual brief sighting of a creature and experienced a powerful vocalization, plus they gathered extensive witness detail and physical evidence.

The plan was to set out the next day for Texas. Charlie had gotten a text the week before from friend and fellow bigfooter Sarah Whitson, who reported a recent sighting south of Texarkana, not all that far away.

Despite the unglamorous parking lot ambience and intermittent traffic noise, Charlie and Betty were plenty fatigued, and slept well this night. An up-close run-in with an eight-foot monster will do that.

3

LONE STAR SNAKE SLING

The next morning, Charlie and Betty got an early start on the Texas segment of their trip. They took Rt. 3 east toward Arkansas, then drove south on US-271 and TX-77 east to Rt. 59 in far northeast Texas. It was a hot, dry stretch of road on this early September day, but fortunately, total travel time was only a couple of hours.

Motor Myrtle rolled to a stop in the small town of Atlanta, Texas for breakfast on Rt. 59. There, Charlie got an order of McDonald's pancakes and sausage with coffee, and afterward, Betty got to enjoy a few chunks of sausage left over from the Golden Arches morning meal.

Next, the peripatetic pals continued heading southwest to the Lake o' the Pines State Park area. Charlie had arranged to meet the next witness, a 45-(or so)-year-old man named Jim Morton, on the grounds of that park, along with SSDD member Sarah Whitson.

Later, Motor Myrtle would likely have an overnight stay somewhere within the park grounds.

An experienced sasquatch investigator, Sarah Whitson had a unique talent of which Charlie had been well aware for several years. She was a skilled and perceptive wildlife artist who, after discussing encounters with witnesses, would produce sketches of the creatures that the individuals had seen. Adding an illustrative element to the assembled evidence, Sarah's skills enabled her to inhabit a unique and valuable roost in the bigfoot investigative community.

The three people had agreed to meet at the Cedar Springs Park and boat ramp inside the park perimeter. The facilities were surrounded by a plethora of pine trees that towered over everything in the area. Charlie steered Motor Myrtle into the parking lot, and a man got out of his pickup truck and walked somewhat hesitantly toward the RV. Charlie was quite sure who this would be.

Stepping down out of the tall vehicle, Charlie inquired of the fair-skinned, strawberry blonde man in jeans and t-shirt, "Greetings, sir, would you be Mr. Morton?"

"Yes, that's right. Are you Charlie?" asked Jim Morton with a polite but vaguely nervous tone.

"One and the same, and this is Ms. Betty, my intrepid navigator and supervisor," Charlie said, motioning to the front windshield of the RV, where Betty was watching the proceedings from above.

"I guess it's always good to have a traveling companion," commented Jim. "I always take my yellow lab when I go out fishing, but I didn't want him out here again where the...stuff... happened," he added. With this statement he pursed his lips and shook his head just a bit, indicating to Charlie that the man's encounter with a sasquatch may not have occurred without generating a measure of discomfort.

Soon, another car drove up and parked next to Motor Myrtle. It was clearly Sarah Whitson, a thin, pretty woman with sharp features. She sported long, straight brunette hair with generous bangs on her forehead, and an earthy overall vibe. She got out of her car and walked up to Charlie and Jim.

"Hi there, Charlie, it's been a few years," she said jauntily as she gave him a big, enthusiastic hug. Betty barked once from inside the vehicle as her master was suddenly smooched by another woman.

"Oh, Sarah, you remain a vision if ever there was one," said Charlie as he politely looked Sarah over from top to bottom. She was wearing long camo pants, a black tank top and hiking boots. She looked like she was altogether ready for a Texas creature quest.

"How is Francesca these days?" she asked Charlie.

"Oh, she's chockfull of her faculties, and as spunky and demanding as ever," Charlie replied gleefully.

"And this is Mr. Jim Morton," Charlie added, gesturing toward Jim. "As you know, Jim was fortunate enough to have directly encountered a sasquatch on these very park grounds."

"Um, *fortunate* enough..." echoed Jim distantly while looking first at Sarah and then at Charlie. Clearly he didn't concur with Charlie's positive characterization of the monster encounter. "I could have probably done without what me and my boy saw that day," he said with a palpable hint of gloominess.

"Well, regardless, it's great to meet you, Jim," said Sarah, kindly extending a hand that Jim shook gently.

"Ah yes," chimed in Charlie, "your son was with you on the road that day, I'm now reminded."

"Uh huh, he was with me" replied Jim, "I think he's in even worse shape over the event than I am."

All was quiet for a few moments.

Then Charlie piped up and asked of Jim, "Well, can you please show us the location where the encounter took place?"

"Sure," began Jim, "It's not far from here, but I don't think I want to linger there too long. What we saw was just unbelievable," he added.

"I'd be glad to drive," offered Sarah quite quickly and eagerly.

The three people got into Sarah's red SUV and headed down the main park road.

The Lake o' the Pines park was a deeply wooded sanctuary for recreational activities and many types of wildlife, offering great fishing in the large, well-known reservoir. Tall pine and deciduous trees closely lined the edge of the paved roadway, very nearly creating a dark green tunnel through this beautiful wilderness area.

The investigative trio had driven for just two or three minutes when Jim spoke up.

"Do you see this next rise in the road?" he asked. "That's where we saw the creature."

Sarah pulled off to the gravel shoulder of the road and stopped the vehicle. Everyone stepped out of the SUV. In this instance, Charlie had left Betty back in the RV so that he could better focus on the witness account.

Although this was a sunny day, the tall, thick trees blocked much of the sunlight, and almost the entire area was in shadow.

Charlie had his laptop and he was about to set it on the hood of the SUV when he caught himself, looked at Sarah and said, "Do you mind?"

She replied, "Sure, you can set it on there."

Charlie did so, then observed Jim looking around the area from side to side.

"This is it," Jim said to the others simply.

Charlie said, "Okay then, please tell us about what happened here, Jim."

Jim continued looking intently all around the shadowed area, perhaps, as Charlie surmised, assessing the level of safety at this moment—precisely where he had seen such a disturbing sight recently. Jim appeared to be staring off into the deep green forest, scanning from one side to the other for potential woodland beasts of excessive proportions.

Returning to the anticipated topic, Jim said, "My son Trevor and I came out here to do some fishing, along with my yellow lab Joey."

"As we were coming down off this little hill," said Jim, "I saw a black bear right in the middle of the road, facing away from the vehicle. I slowed down the truck and came to a stop right away because seeing a bear in the middle of the road is *not* something that happens here too much... and you certainly don't want to run into it."

"Bears are rare in this area," he continued. "I've heard stories of them being around here, but I've never seen one. In fact, I *still* haven't seen one."

Charlie found the latter statement a tad puzzling but decided not to comment pending subsequent information from Jim.

During Jim's retelling of his account, the trio walked down the slight grade in the road and reached the bottom of the small hill.

"So I stopped the truck here so we could observe the bear safely. Trevor is 15," said Jim, "and I thought it would be a great opportunity for him to see some rare wildlife."

Trevor was in the front passenger seat of the truck when Jim sighted the creature.

"You know, I wanted to be really careful because a bear—or something else that big—can take you down in a hurry. So I wanted Trevor to experience this creature but not get too close to it."

"The weird thing is that as we were looking at this bear crouched down over something," said Jim, "the bear stood up, turned around and looked right at us. But as soon as I took one full look at the creature standing there, I knew it wasn't a bear."

Jim reported a deep feeling of shock washing over him as he realized he was seeing something more than unusual.

Trevor apparently just said, "Um, Dad..."

Joey commented as well, pushing out a sturdy, deep bark as he looked forward at the creature from inside the truck cab.

Instead of a bear, however, this was a huge dark creature standing upright and tall on two legs. Jim estimated the creature's height at between eight and ten feet, and nearly four feet wide at the chest and shoulders. It was truly massive.

According to Jim, the creature had a large head with dark eyes, either dark brown or black, a large flat nose, and a face that was a bit lighter in color than the body. Although it was quite dark in this thickly tree-lined section of roadway, Jim perceived that the animal (clearly by now a bigfoot) was not fully black as he had at first thought, but perhaps a very dark brown, and its hair, covering the whole body except for parts of the face, was at least four inches long.

The creature's limbs were huge and clearly muscular, and the upper body came down to a V as do big bodybuilders and some football players, said Jim. He estimated the creature's fists to be at around the size of "a canned ham." He reported this observation because one of the creature's hands was closed into a fist and had something in it. The head was somewhat conical in shape, and very little neck was visible.

With the truck stopped and the windows open—with father, son and dog clearly incredulous at what they were seeing—the creature continued to look at them, then roared at them so loudly and deeply that they could feel its vibration as it pounded into the vehicle and into their chests. In reaction to the blast of terrifying noise, Joey tried unsuccessfully to hide underneath the truck's bench seat.

Next, appearing to take careful aim, the bigfoot actually threw what it had in its hand at the truck! Whatever the dark squiggly object was, it flew a few feet above the truck and went some distance behind it, and back up the hilly pavement.

During all of this time, Trevor had been imploring his father to turn around and drive away. The boy was utterly terrified. Jim turned the truck around to drive back toward where the thrown object landed in the road behind them.

The son did *not* want the father to stop after turning around and was begging him to flee the area in the vehicle as fast as possible.

"Dad, we have to get out of here!" he screamed to his father.

"I know, I know," said Jim. "Just wait a minute."

As the truck approached the flung object and the father got out quickly to investigate, he walked up to it and realized that it was a deceased cottonmouth snake. (Jim was an experienced fisherman and woodsman, quickly recognizing the venomous species.) In anger, the huge creature had thrown the snake at the humans!

Jim figured that the creature may have either killed the snake or it had already been lying dead on the wooded road. Not sure about what to do given this very odd development, Jim tossed the snake remains into the back of his pickup and hurried back to the cab so the group could rapidly exit the area.

Just then, without warning, the creature began powerfully running toward the truck and its now totally-terrified occupants.

Trevor screamed out, "Dad, *go*!!!"

The bigfoot got within about twenty feet of the truck before Jim had it in gear and peeled out in reverse. A hundred or so yards down the road, he fishtailed the truck around and drove off in a frontward direction.

Looking in his rear view mirror, Jim saw the creature give up the chase and break off to one side of the road. In Jim's last view of it, the creature was striding up a hill into the deeper woods at, by Jim's account, seeming otherworldly speed.

The entire creature encounter happened very fast, apparently. It took less than a minute of elapsed time.

Jim and Trevor both were quite shaken by the encounter, and they didn't stop the vehicle until they were all the way home.

"My goodness," said Sarah to Jim. "Have you ever had someone or something throw a snake at you?!"

"No, this was definitely a first," replied Jim. "And the bigfoot creature was so enormously big that it kind of propelled my mind into some sort of parallel space. It's hard to describe, but the massiveness of this creature, plus the fact that it slung a serpent through the air at me, was certainly the strangest thing I've experienced in my life."

Everyone was hushed and reflective for several moments.

Charlie then felt compelled to inquire about an item of trivia: "Jim, do you know what became of the low-luck serpent after this event?"

Jim guffawed mildly and said, "I think back home, Joey snatched it out of the truck bed. After that, who knows?"

More silence ensued as the group pondered the slung snake's fate.

"So Jim, can you point out to us the exact spot where you saw the bigfoot?" asked Charlie, returning to more relevant concerns.

"Sure, it's right down here."

Still gripped by Jim's recounting of the tale, all three humans walked slowly down to a low spot in the road.

Jim stood exactly where his truck had stopped on the day of the sighting, and he pointed to where the bigfoot creature was initially crouched down and then stood fully upright. He also pointed out the location where the airborne snake had landed.

Charlie corralled his camera and took photos of the site from various angles, then walked to where the father indicated the sasquatch had stood in the middle of the road. While taking photos, Charlie had to dodge a few cars (virtually bullfighter style) as they rolled through this sunlight-starved portion of the park.

Looking back toward Jim and Sarah now, Charlie began raising a hand up above his own head, and yelled to Jim to tell him when his hand was approximately at the level of the bigfoot's head. Charlie continued to elevate his hand up, up and up, to the very extremes of how high his arm could reach, and could go no further. Jim said, "Somewhere around there, I think. Probably higher."

This creature was clearly immense in scale. "You know, I do believe I injured myself with that expansive vertical reach," commented Charlie in an aside to Sarah, who snickered a little at the description.

"And that's not a very reliable height estimation scheme anyway," added Charlie.

He then walked back to where Jim and Sarah were standing. By this time Sarah was interviewing Jim in great detail regarding the proportions and coloration of the features observed on the creature. She drew on a sketch pad she had been carrying, creating rough recreations of Jim's impressions of the creature. Sarah quickly did both a facial close-up and a full body sketch rendition of the huge bigfoot.

Jim was quite cooperative in reporting his observances, though clearly still somewhat unnerved at what had happened recently at that very location. Charlie noticed that Jim kept looking up into the hills along this dark section of road, apparently wondering if the huge creature might still be in the vicinity.

Sarah was able to get enough visual data down on paper to support the more refined, later versions of her sketches.

After continuing with their back-and-forth discussion of the encounter details, Charlie and Sarah both thanked Jim profusely for his thorough description and impressions of the event. They both shook hands with Jim and wished him well.

The trio walked back to Sarah's car, she turned it around and they headed back to the parking lot where the other vehicles remained. Jim said his goodbyes, walked to his truck and departed the lot—likely with a sense of relief about leaving.

Charlie and Sarah stood next to Motor Myrtle talking some more about the witness and his bigfoot account. Charlie let Betty out of the RV and took her for a leisurely stroll around the lovely area. Sarah accompanied them.

On their group walk, Charlie brought up a highly pertinent topic.

"You know, Sarah, I'm entirely famished after having heard Mr. Morton's account," he said, "and not necessarily because of the tasty snake aspect. I am, however, aware of the tasty catfish that this area's known for. Would you care to join me in a fishy restaurant repast?"

"That might just be delightful," replied Sarah with a smile.

And the lunch date was on.

Getting back into their respective vehicles, Charlie and Sarah drove toward the nearby town of Ore City. They had lunch at

Sadie's Catfish World, an informal eatery where the house specialty was no mystery to prospective customers.

Over luxurious fried lunches (catfish for Charlie, shrimp for Sarah) accompanied by hush puppies, the two veteran bigfooters traded notes about sightings in their respective experience of late.

At the table, Sarah asked Charlie about his forthcoming plans. "So what's next for you on your monster quest?"

"I'm heading to Louisiana next, it seems, since I believe I have a date with a massive swamp monster there," he said.

"Oh, there's *nothing* better than a good swamp monster to break up the monotony," said Sarah.

Charlie added, "And after that I'll be befriending monsters up the East Coast, and perhaps as far up as Michigan."

"Wow," replied Sarah. "How does Francesca feel about all this?"

Charlie took a big bite of catfish before replying. "Well," he began, "I'd say she's somewhat crestfallen at the prospect of remaining behind while I tangle with assorted forest giants. But she knows this is pretty important to me. And who knows: I'll probably bring her along next time."

Afterward in the catfish parking lot, Sarah and Charlie said goodbye to each other and enjoyed one more affectionate hug. Sarah got in her SUV and headed home. Charlie drove his RV to a campground site back at Lake o' the Pines.

Later that night, Charlie finished documenting all of his findings on his laptop for submission to the SSDD. He consulted his SSDD itinerary and reviewed the particulars of what would be his next investigative target: the Honey Island Swamp Monster near St. Tammany Parish, Louisiana.

After RV bedtime for Charlie and Betty, a Texas-sized thunderstorm brewed up over the park, buffeting Motor Myrtle with pounding rain, fearsome lightning and rumbling thunder. Betty burrowed deeply into the covers, plastering herself against Charlie's legs as she sought cuddly comfort from the raging storm outside. The huddled RV dwellers were suddenly cognizant of and thankful for quality vehicle construction that could keep the violent elements at bay tonight.

Several weeks later, Charlie received a highly anticipated email from Sarah. Attached to the email were the two final witness sketch images Sarah had done of the gigantic snake-tossing Lake o' the Pines bigfoot.

The facial close-up was a stunning portrait of a serious, slightly menacing monster visage with large, dark, piercing eyes, a prominent brow ridge, a large, mostly flat nose, and dark hair flowing down off of a pointed head toward hugely wide shoulders.

In Sarah's full-body sketch, the massive bigfoot has one huge hand down at its side. However, the opposing hand grips the remains of the late, unfortunate, soon-to-be-airborne serpent. Charlie could barely stop staring in awe at this composite image that was unlike any other in the world of terrestrial creatures.

4

OLD STUMPY STRIKES AGAIN

Charlie and Betty's next stop on their itinerary would occur well into the neighboring state of Louisiana. Charlie always loved Louisiana (particularly New Orleans), as he and his wife Francesca had visited periodically over the years to enjoy colorful seafood from the bayous, rivers and the Gulf, along with a bit of intemperate alcoholic decadence, plus a smattering of history gleaned from numerous landmarks they visited throughout the region.

The current trip, however, would be in the province of Charlie's *other* girl, Betty, and the carousing would likely be limited to samplings of a few local fried flavors.

From Texas, Charlie steered Motor Myrtle east on I-20 to I-49 south (below Shreveport). They stayed on that route and drove southeast for several hours. They then took US 190 directly east to the large city of Baton Rouge, where they stopped for a late lunch at a little Creole bistro.

As Betty napped in the RV, Charlie had succulent, steaming crawfish étouffée (served over rice), bread in a skillet and a cup of seafood gumbo. He left with a small doggy bag of redfish and a few gumbo extracts for his RV traveling companion. Betty was very appreciative of the rouge fishy bites.

In Baton Rouge, I-90 transitioned into I-12 east, which the travelers took to an area right above the huge, famous Lake Pontchartrain—about a six-hour drive in all.

Charlie and Betty were headed toward an area known as the Honey Island Swamp, located northeast of Lake Pontchartrain. The swamp is a large wilderness area containing a plethora of animal life including alligators, feral hogs, nutria, snakes, egrets, black bears, eagles and even a legendary creature (purportedly): the Honey Island Swamp Monster.

Having previously accessed a SSDD report of a bigfoot sighting in the area, Charlie had no idea if the creature witnessed recently had anything to do with the area's monster legend, but he was certainly going to look into it.

After stopping at a Winn-Dixie to stock up on supplies, Charlie and Betty pulled into the Pearl River WMA (Wildlife Management Area) campgrounds in St. Tammany Parish. Charlie hooked up the 30-amp power (via a 50-to-30-amp adapter), water and other connections.

The forest cover there varied from numerous cypress trees (including aged cypress giants under which you could park an RV), stands of hardwood deciduous trees (e.g., live oak, pecan, hickory, beech, magnolia, etc.), and wetter marshland to the south.

In the middle of the travelers' first night at the campground, Charlie awoke to the unwelcome sound of Betty scratching at the RV door. Charlie stumbled out of a deep sleep and quickly realized that nature was calling his canine. He walked outside with Betty on leash and waited while she expelled into the grass whatever extent of fishy leftovers did not track with her tummy at St. Tammany. Ah, the glamour of pooch parenthood.

As he waited for Betty to complete her hurl by the Pearl River, Charlie let his mind wander to the late-morning appointment he had established for the next day with a local man, Andrew Davis, who had a recent, very unusual encounter with a bigfoot-type creature at water's edge.

Although it was early September and summer would be over soon, it was darn hot and sticky on this day. This wasn't at all unusual in Louisiana.

Mr. Davis gave Charlie directions to a spot where he had gone out to fish along the Old Pearl River, which runs through the large swamp. After an intentionally mild cereal and kibble breakfast, Charlie and Betty drove to the Pearl River access that Mr. Davis had specified, and they met him there.

Andrew was a handsome late-30-something Black man who was around six feet in height, by Charlie's estimation. (Charlie was no six-footer.) He wore a pair of jeans and a crisp white t-shirt along with a baseball cap and trendy sunglasses.

Having already parked his truck, Andrew politely met Charlie and Betty once the two travelers had climbed down out of the RV, with Betty on leash.

"So, you're Monsieur Andrew Davis, correct?" asked Charlie, clumsily attempting to reproduce a French Cajun dialect.

"Ah oui, you can call me Drew. And you're Charlie Marlowe, right?" Drew asked of Charlie. "A French Cajun not from this area?" he queried humorously.

"Indeed, vraiment!" exclaimed Charlie heartily in partial, garbled French. "And this attractive young mademoiselle is Betty," Charlie added as Betty walked over to Mr. Davis to solicit some affectionate petting. She stood up with her front paws landing on Drew's legs above the knees.

"I'm quite fond of beagles," said Drew as he rubbed Betty's ears, "and this one will surely like the seafood around here."

"She already does, I'm afraid," replied Charlie. "She's already wheedled some local delicacies out of me."

"Yes, these hounds can be pretty persuasive when they get hungry," said Andrew. "I've got a crazy hound who actually ate one of my sidewalk lights the other day."

"My, that is a...an enlightening display of appetite indeed," said Charlie in reaction.

"And if you don't mind my asking," said Charlie with a quick follow-up, "what is that rather odd-looking creature residing on your ball cap?"

Drew giggled slightly and shook his head. "A number of years ago, they renamed the minor league baseball club here from the New Orleans Zephyrs to the Baby Cakes. Nobody knows why," he said dryly. "Then, the team moved out a few years ago, and I think they took their snarling, angry baby with them," he added, pointing to the king/cherub-like animated figure on the front of his dark ball cap.

"You have my sympathies, I suppose," replied Charlie with some befuddlement.

Changing the subject a bit, Charlie asked Drew to show him where his sighting occurred.

The riverside area where today's meeting took place was lush with vegetation. Spanish moss hung down abundantly from countless big cypress trees. Many cypress branches hung out over the river, and the droopy, slightly spooky moss nearly reached down to the water level.

Of course, with this being a swamp, dark water was everywhere. Although a visitor could readily walk along the shore of the river, most of the substantial travel in this area was done by flat-bottom tour boat, kayak or low-slung bass boat—used mostly by local fishermen.

A fisherman himself, it seemed, Drew started describing his monster encounter.

To begin with he told Charlie that the day of the encounter was a cloudy, somewhat misty day. He had walked just a few minutes with his gear, looking for a preferable fishing spot.

As he made his way along the river and toward the bank where he decided to drop his line, Drew heard a splash to his right but couldn't see the origin of the noise around some trees.

Moved to investigate, Drew went around a slight bend in the river where the bank jutted out and formed somewhat of a point. As Drew got around the corner, he suddenly observed a huge, dark man standing in the water just off the bank. Andrew estimated he was about 50 or 60 yards away from the bipedal individual standing in the water.

The large figure was covered in grayish black hair from top to bottom. Drew thought he almost looked like a living cypress tree, with flowing hair hanging well down off of his body. He was very muscular, with long, shaggy arms, and looked tall even though his legs were mostly underwater.

After watching the individual for less than 30 seconds, Drew was then astounded to observe the man (or creature) bend down and forcibly pull a large cypress stump completely out of the mud. Lifting with both arms, the creature hoisted the massive wet brown chunk over its head, heaved back and threw the stump five or six yards forward out into the river. The creature emitted a heavy, deep grunt as it tossed the stump...somewhat like a massive shot putter in a field event.

With water dripping from it as it flew, the stump created an utterly titanic, deeply noisy splash that sent powerful ripples of water far out into the river.

Drew remembered standing in absolute awe of what he had just seen. First of all, this was clearly not a human being that he was close to and observing, even though the creature was standing on two legs and was essentially human-shaped. That in itself was hugely shocking to Drew. But additionally, for someone to have the strength and coordination to dislodge a submerged tree stump from the dark water and be able to lift it overhead and toss it well out into the river—was an act of absolutely superhuman power.

Drew reported simply standing frozen in place upon observing the creature's positively miraculous act of physical strength. At once, all of the familiar surrounding sounds of the forest and river—predominantly bird calls—ceased.

Drew said that after several quiet seconds, he was wholly dismayed to see the creature turn slowly away from the river, to looking to its left...straight at Drew. He guessed that the creature may have picked up his scent, as Drew certainly wasn't making any noise to attract attention. At that point he estimated the creature's height to be at least seven feet. The being's facial features weren't clear at this distance.

Unsure about what was going to happen next, Drew was relieved to see that the creature soon turned and walked away, parallel to the river, to Drew's right. He moved rather quickly and did not look back.

Still very much in shock, Drew reported that he had walked in an admittedly unsteady fashion back to his truck to gather his thoughts and try to calm down after the encounter. Having done so over a period of about 15 minutes, he then returned with great caution to the spot where he had seen the huge creature.

There he observed several gigantic bare footprints along the water. He estimated them at maybe 15 or 16 inches in length. He took pictures of the prints with his phone before leaving the area.

Charlie felt compelled to comment summarily on Drew's experience, saying emphatically, "What you saw was an undoubtedly unique and amazing sight, Mr. Davis."

"Yes, we've all heard the monster tales from around here, but I never expected to see one...not in my wildest dreams," replied Drew in a slightly downcast fashion.

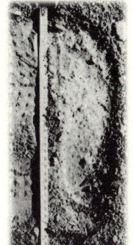

After recounting his tale, Drew led Charlie and Betty to the spot where the creature had stood on the bank. Charlie looked closely at the ground in that spot, saw what remained of the footprints, and was able to follow them for a bit down the riverside. The impressions in the relatively soft mud were deep, although not well defined after the passage of some time.

Still holding Betty on leash and now grappling with his tape measure, Charlie measured the clearest of the footprints at just under 16 inches in length, and he took a number of photos of track and tape measure.

While the group continued to check out the site, Drew now spotted the bulging clear eyes, large snout and bounteous body scales of an apparently large, greenish-gray alligator in the water several yards off of the bank. The threatening creature was swimming steadily toward the shore.

"Friends, we've got some king-size company here," said Drew urgently to Charlie and Betty.

Charlie looked in the direction that Drew was focused on, and quickly said, "My goodness, this is an unwelcome development!"

Charlie was suddenly quite glad that he had kept Betty on her leash this whole time.

As the gator (easily a 7-footer) hit the shore, it quickly displayed its amphibious chops, continuing with a shuffle swiftly up onto solid ground and heading toward Charlie, Drew and Betty, with spiky teeth easily visible—even though its mouth was closed. Betty was likely an appetizing target for this reptilian monster. Everyone turned and ran without delay.

After retreating about 20 feet straight back from the water, the trio turned and began running parallel to the shoreline in the direction from which they had originally come, toward their vehicles. There was no dawdling amidst this gator-scape.

The gator continued to follow the group but wasn't as fast a runner as the two fearful humans and canine. It stopped after pursuing them about 50 feet.

The humans and dog, however, did not stop. They all continued at a fairly rapid run until they got back to the parking area. All three individuals turned and looked backward at certain points along the way, hoping that the big rumbling reptile had run its route. Soon, it had, apparently.

They stopped running just prior to getting to Motor Myrtle, where the two men bent over and struggled to catch their breath. Betty continued to look back in the direction of the toothy river monster.

Drew said quite evenly, "I'm afraid my days of conquering the 400 meters are quite a bit behind me."

Struggling mightily to recover his wind, Charlie added with a huff, "My days of conquering the 400 *centimeters* weren't even particularly good." Drew smiled with amusement at this self-deprecating crack.

Charlie opened the entrance door to the RV, went in and returned with a bowl of water for Betty, and some cold bottled waters for Drew and himself.

Drew and Charlie leaned with their backs against the recreational vehicle, got themselves rehydrated, and continued to talk for some time about not only today's crocodilian clash but also about Drew's prior sasquatch sighting. Drew patiently answered Charlie's many questions about the huge swamp monster and its instigation of a soaring, splashing stump.

Eventually, Charlie thanked Drew for his time, and Drew gave Betty some friendly pats before walking over to his truck and driving away from the area. Charlie and Betty reentered Motor Myrtle where Charlie set about organizing his notes and photos from the day.

It was now late afternoon, so the dynamic duo headed in Motor Myrtle to find a restaurant that served items like gumbo, jambalaya and po' boy dinner delicacies. They settled on a seafood restaurant and market where Charlie got a shrimp po' boy and seafood gumbo, and Betty (afterward) got a to-go small order of catfish off the kids' menu. Charlie hoped the food stayed down this time.

Other than being happy to find the great local seafood, Charlie was pleased to have found that the Honey Island Swamp Monster—or perhaps a relative of same—definitely existed and resided somewhere in the area. His witness had seen it, and Charlie had documented its swampy tracks before an insolent alligator crashed the party.

Not in any particular hurry to exit the area, Charlie, the next morning, called and reserved a ticket for a swamp tour of Honey Island by boat. After arriving at the tour landing and cruising the gift shop until launch time, Charlie boarded one of the flat-bottomed boats with ten or so other tourists.

The pilot, Captain Broussard, was a stocky, genial, witty local man of retirement age—like Charlie, with a substantial touch of Cajun accent to his speaking voice. After backing away from the dock, he slowly guided the boat through the serpentine bayou channels full of low-hanging cypress trees and told stories while pointing out many examples of local wildlife. He was full of corny jokes and puns, and interspersed some clearly tall tales into his nautical narrative.

The floating group spotted a few herons and egrets, swamp hogs, turtles, and frogs soaking up sun on the banks and downed logs of the Old Pearl River. The kids on board clearly loved the rare sights of local creatures.

One of the highlights of these types of Louisiana tours was the proximity of gators—although viewed from the relative safety of a boat. On this muggy but bright morning, the captain tossed some small marshmallows from the vessel out into the water. Sure enough, after a few minutes, several gators large and small began to assemble in the water in order to nab some sweet treats.

Charlie got to hold a captain-supplied stick with an impaled marshmallow out over the water as a medium-sized gator approached silently...and somewhat ominously. As the gator got about three feet from the side of the boat, it swiftly reared up out of the water, gobbled Charlie's mallow off the stick, and hit the water again with a robust splash on the way down. Kids on the boat squealed with a combination of fright and delight whenever this occurred.

At one point a "rival" flatboat full of tourists approached Captain Broussard's vessel from the opposite direction. Both wearing knowing smiles, the respective skippers briefly engaged in some bayou battle—in the form of marshmallow missiles flung at the opposing tour boat. Many more giggles ensued. Nearby alert gators scooped up and devoured the detritus of the watery war.

Charlie found the entire bayou experience quite relaxing and fun—a salubrious contrast to his more tense interfaces with traumatized witnesses who had run into unescorted giant primates recently.

Although Charlie wasn't on an evidence hunt while on the swamp boat, he certainly kept his eyes peeled for wildlife on the banks and in the water, occasionally pointing out to the other tourists what he'd spotted. He particularly enjoyed seeing and photographing huge white egrets with long yellow beaks at river's edge. (They were hard to miss due to their bright coloring.)

Over the course of the two-hour-or-so swamp tour, Charlie took many pictures of both flora and fauna unique to this unusual and beautiful environment before heading back to shore.

The road warriors stopped at a seafood buffet restaurant for lunch and enjoyed a sampling of boiled crawfish, shrimp, blue crabs, oysters, fried flounder and speckled trout. They then returned in Motor Myrtle to the Pearl River WMA campground for the afternoon and overnight hours.

Early in the evening, Charlie put a call in to Francesca back home before it got too late; our travelers were an hour ahead of the Mountain time zone, where Santa Fe was located.

Francesca was happy to hear from Charlie. She asked him lots of questions about how well he was taking care of himself. In general Charlie said he was doing well, but that both he and his traveling companion were taking in copious calories up to this point on the southern swing of the trip.

At one point Charlie told Francesca that at least he was able to download some of the calories to gators.

"Gators?!" asked Francesca with some surprise.

It was clear that Charlie would need to more fully explain this unusual comment to Francesca.

"I was minding my own business on a boat during a swamp tour," began Charlie, "and the boat captain told those on the starboard side that various underprivileged alligators in the area had a powerful yen for marshmallows. So, we obliged and fed the monsters some mallows," he concluded.

"You fed marshmallows to alligators?" asked Francesca with mock concern. "I'm sure those are nothing but empty calories to those reptiles."

"That may be so, but *you* try denying sweet treats to a huge lizard coming straight toward you; it behooves one to deliver the requisite delicacy post-haste."

"Well, please don't exchange your core mission of bigfooting for the pursuit of obviously-over-spoiled alligators," said Francesca.

"That's a fully unlikely scenario," concluded Charlie.

Later, on the grounds of the motor home park, Charlie took Betty for a walk through the beautiful, grassy, wooded, riverside park area. Betty enjoyed stretching her legs and spotting an occasional swamp bird at which she could bark.

Before turning in that night, Charlie returned to his documentation efforts and reviewed his itinerary for the next witness visit. The location was in far northeast Florida, and Myrtle would head out in the morning. They had yet another seven-hour drive in front of them.

Rolling out after a frozen pancake breakfast (brought from home then microwaved), they took I-10 east for the bulk of the day, crossed into Florida, and eventually hit FL 125 north to the town of Taylor.

5

Juvies And Jalopies

Some weeks before, a rather renowned bigfoot investigator named John Preen had sent Charlie an email briefly describing an unusual bigfoot encounter that had been reported directly to him from the very northern portion of Florida. This area was adjacent to the Osceola National Forest, the Osceola Wildlife Management Area and the John M. Bethea State Forest.

Although there apparently wasn't any available physical evidence specific to this event, Charlie's intent was to travel there (if feasible at the indicated time) and do additional detailed follow-up with the witnesses involved. As usual, it was likely that their verbal accounts could shed more light on the incident than their brief initial written report.

Heading due east, Motor Myrtle traversed the remainder of Louisiana on I-10 amidst a lengthy cruise that largely maintained the same latitude throughout. The travelers headed through the far southeastern tip of Mississippi and across the similarly nether regions of southern Alabama. Their destination was well up on the Florida Panhandle.

Along the way they stopped for lunch in Mobile. At a trendy-looking brownstone bistro on Dauphin Street, Charlie had a smoked tuna salad sandwich with a hash-brown casserole side. It was suitably comforting and yummy. Betty eagerly welcomed him when he returned to the rig. As Charlie entered the vehicle, Betty stood up high on her back legs and bounced in anticipation of some tasty leftovers. She offered no discernable complaints about the smoked tuna treat.

Crossing through Florida later in the day, Motor Myrtle took Florida highway 121 north at the town of Macclenny, nearly to the southern tip of Georgia. The recent bigfoot encounter had occurred in the town of Taylor, Florida. The totality of the drive to the small town east of Jacksonville took more than six hours. As usual, Charlie was plenty fatigued upon reaching his lodging destination, Macclenny.

The travelers pulled into a nearby RV campground, St. Mary's Cove, which was nicely wooded and had a beautiful riverside white-sandy beach. As Charlie experienced during other stops on this southern swing, the mid-September weather was a bit sultry.

After checking in and hooking up the RV in the early evening, Charlie took Betty for a long walk across the grounds adjoining the picturesque river. Remarkably, a rooster was strolling about the grounds, and Betty took immediate and vociferous interest in the lone leghorn. As usual, Charlie had to hold back the dog as she chafed to charge the chunky, funky chicken.

After a quiet night within Motor Myrtle's friendly confines, Charlie and Betty awoke to grab breakfast—microwaved oatmeal for Charlie, and kibble with gravy and green beans for Betty. The artificial though fragrant smell of the maple and brown sugar oatmeal filled the RV as the travelers got ready for their day.

Charlie telephoned the witness in Taylor to confirm their meeting that morning, and the group headed out, picking up Florida 125 north along the far eastern edge of the Osceola Wildlife Management Area.

Charlie drove with Betty to the address the witness had provided. They pulled up to a low-slung, tan-colored, single story shingle-roofed brick home. Numerous leafy trees and even some cypress ringed the property. The flat front yard contained many shrubs and a few medium-sized fruit trees. This was a nice, green, shady spot on a bright sunny day.

One of the unusual aspects of this case was that the apparent witness was a child, whose parents originally reported the sighting to the well-known Mr. Preen. Charlie would be meeting with the parents and possibly the child, and he brought Betty along just in case her presence might help relax the youngster and help him or her more freely share information.

Charlie parked the RV, walked up to the house with Betty on leash and rang the doorbell. A fairly young man, likely in his early- to mid-30s, with a stocky build (like Charlie) and a flip of generous brown hair at his shoulders, opened the front door.

"Good morning, I'm Charlie Marlowe," offered Charlie without delay, reaching out to shake the man's hand. "And this is Betty."

"Hello, Mr. Marlowe, I'm Sean Williams and this is my wife Carole," said Sean, politely motioning to his wife who had just walked into the small foyer.

"Please call me Charlie. Is it okay if Betty accompanies me in?" he asked.

"Certainly, Charlie," said Carole, a somewhat tall, thin woman with long blonde hair flowing down her back. "Is this your first time in the area?"

"Oh most definitely," replied Charlie in an animated fashion. "I live in the high desert of New Mexico, where these beautiful cypress trees only appear in idle daydreams," he said in a very nearly poetic manner.

"Well, we've got all *kinds* of trees here, Charlie, and lots *of* them," explained Carole. "It stays hot and stuffy well into autumn 'round these parts, but at least we've got some shade to cool things down a bit." Like her husband, Carole spoke in a slow, deeply southern cadence.

Dressed in khaki shorts, a blue horizontal striped polo shirt and white tennis shoes, Carole seemed quite friendly and outgoing, while Charlie sensed that Sean was a bit more reserved in nature. No matter.

From the foyer, the group walked to their right into a sizeable living room.

"Have a seat anywhere, Charlie," said Sean quietly.

Seeking suitable seating, Charlie looked around the room which was fronted by a large bay window that let in abundant sunlight. He spotted a heavy wooden rocker in one corner of the room and plunked himself down where he could both comfortably rock and dutifully gather evidence. He pulled his laptop from his bag and began setting it up. Betty lay down next to him on the living room's large brown braided rug.

Carole and Sean sat next to each other on a puffy gray couch directly across from Charlie.

"Oh yeah, bud, would you like some water, a soda or a beer?" asked Sean.

Charlie thought for a moment, considered the time of day, and replied, "Well, maybe some water would fit the bill, thank you."

Sean got up and walked around the corner, likely to the kitchen.

Meanwhile Carole asked, "So, do you know much about what happened here, Charlie?"

Charlie considered the question. "Only a general sketch of the events," he replied as Sean promptly returned with a cold bottle of water and a small plastic bowl, probably intended for Betty's use. Charlie opened the bottle and poured a generous splash of water for Betty, who began lapping up the liquid. He set his own water bottle on an adjacent coffee table.

"Well, it seems that our son Wesley, who's nine years old, had quite the experience. And by the way, he's currently upstairs playing in his room," said Carole, pointing to the stairway at the edge of the living room.

"Anyway, on the afternoon of the incident," continued Carole, "Sean and I were in the kitchen. Wesley walked in from the living room pretty worked up, and asked us to follow him out to the front door. Wesley said that there was a little monster standing on the front porch. Sean and I gave each other a pretty twisted look."

Both parents apparently registered disbelief at the boy's statement, but Wesley was insistent that someone should accompany him to the door to see the monster. Sean sluggishly did so while having his hand tugged forcefully by the unrelenting young boy.

Upon getting to the front door behind Wesley, Sean apparently saw nothing unusual. The heavy inner wooden door was wide open and a screen door was closed across the doorway, as was usual during the warm months.

"I don't see anything, little buddy," Sean had said to Wesley.

Wesley became highly agitated, and said, "He was right there on the porch a minute ago!"

Wesley then ran out the front door and started looking around the trees and shrubs in the front yard. Sean watched him from the door, but the boy clearly didn't find anything.

"Come on, Wesley, I think your monster friend is gone," said Sean gently.

Suddenly quite disappointed, Wesley returned to the house.

The incident having ended at that point, Sean and Carole went back to what they were doing in the kitchen at the time. However, in subsequent talks such as over meals and during cleanup and bath times, Wesley insisted that he had seen a figure on the porch. Sean and Carole discussed the urgency of his appeals for several days before reporting the apparent sighting to the noted bigfoot figure, Mr. Preen.

They agreed that as long as they could keep their names from being associated with the report, it wouldn't hurt to add to the region's compendium of monster lore.

Now, Carole called young Wesley down from upstairs to talk with Charlie and visit with Betty.

A small boy with very short brown hair, a friendly, roundish face, and plentiful facial freckles, Wesley shyly came down off the stairs and stepped into the room to join the talk. He was wearing a pair of red shorts and a white t-shirt, with cute suspenders reaching over his shoulders. He wore black sneakers on his feet.

Charlie immediately stood and walked over to the 9-year-old to greet him with a hearty two-fisted yet very gentle handshake.

"Well, how are you today, young man?" Charlie asked warmly and enthusiastically. "I'm Charlie, and my co-detective here is Betty."

"Hi, Charlie and Betty," said Wesley rather quietly, giggling a bit at the canine co-detective reference. He knelt down to scratch Betty's ears, and she licked one side of his face. "We used to have a terrier dog—Tigger—but he got real sick," said Wesley with a slight tone of sadness.

"Oh, I'm sure sorry about that, Wesley," said Charlie in an empathetic manner. Sean and Carole looked on alertly.

"What do you like to do for fun?" asked Charlie in an effort to perk up the boy and elicit his interests.

"Um, I like to play outside a lot," began Wesley, "plus go to the swimming pool, but my favorite game these days is cars."

Without explanation Wesley turned and ran upstairs. Charlie looked quizzically at the parents.

Supplying some explanation, Carole said, "He *really* enjoys his cars."

Just a few seconds later, Wesley returned to the first floor carrying a fairly flat blue box with illustrated race car action on its lid.

Setting the box in the middle of the floor and sitting down with it, Wesley said, "This is my very cool set," as he peeled back the box's lid and proudly displayed an array of colorful metal vehicles of various types including Indy cars, stock cars, muscle cars, pickups, rescue trucks, panel trucks and superhero vehicles.

"That's quite the collection, young man!" said Charlie with genuine admiration. With old knees creaking, he knelt on the floor next to Wesley and asked, "Do you mind if I examine some of them?"

Without hesitation, Wesley replied, "Sure!" He handed Charlie a race car and a tow truck. Charlie inspected them closely, turning them over in his hands and spinning the wheels.

"And these vehicles had something to do with the monster you saw?" asked Charlie, referencing a notable detail from the report that John Preen had submitted.

"Oh yes," replied Wesley energetically. "I think he was *way* interested in my cars."

Charlie let this statement linger for a few seconds before moving on.

He looked over at the parents and asked, "Is it okay if this fine young man gives me a full overview of what he witnessed?"

"Certainly, Charlie," replied Carole. "Go ahead and tell Charlie what you saw, Wesley," she instructed to her son.

The cute, freckle-faced boy looked up at his mother and then back down to his car set, likely gathering his thoughts and memories of that rather unforgettable day.

Charlie repositioned his laptop in preparation for a healthy chunk of evidence gathering.

"I was right here with these cars. I was zooming this old-timey fire truck across the floor to help put out a big fire over at…a building," said Wesley, pointing to the couch upon which his parents were currently sitting.

"As I drove the truck across to the 'building,'" Wesley continued, "I could see out of the corner of my eye that someone was standing on the other side of the screen door watching me."

Wesley continued with a well detailed description of his amazing encounter. "I stopped what I was doing and stood up. I was still carrying my fire truck. At the door was this hairy creature that was somewhere around the same size as me."

At this point, Charlie gently interrupted, asking, "Wesley, what color was the creature's hair, and how long would you say it was?"

Wesley raised a hand to his face and scratched an ear for several moments as he looked at Charlie, who was seated in the rocker typing notes.

"The hair was a little red, or maybe kind of red-brownish," said Wesley thoughtfully. "I guess it was about three inches long in most places, but it wasn't real long all over his face. His face kind of looked like an ape or something."

"An ape, you say?" echoed Charlie.

"Yes, kind of a small ape or some other monkey," said Wesley.

"Can you describe the face?" asked Charlie.

Wesley hesitated to think again, then replied, "I guess the face was kind of flat, with a wide nose. The nose and mouth were kind of light colored. Short hair on the front of his head came down to just above his eyes. I couldn't see his ears; I guess he either didn't have any or they were covered up by hair. There…was some hair on the sides of his face, but not too much. Um, the eyes…were a bit greenish, I guess. They were real big…real bright eyes. And, uh, the lips were pretty much like a person's lips…just flat, mostly. But man, his hair looked *really* cool," concluded Wesley.

"That's wonderful, son," replied Charlie with clear appreciation. Despite Wesley's youth, he was proving to be quite the dependable witness.

Charlie continued. "So, you say he was about your height, right?"

"Yeah, about four foot nothin' or something," said Wesley with a slight snicker. "I'd say he was a kid, like me."

"And was he standing up, just like you and I stand up on two legs?" asked Charlie, attempting to identify the creature's potential bipedal nature versus a quadruped's bodily stance.

"Yeah, he stood there just like me, with one hand up on the screen. If he wasn't so dang ugly and hairy, I guess he could have been my brother," Wesley added, looking over at his parents a bit squeamishly. They both chuckled quietly at this familial reference.

"Was the creature heavy or lightweight, would you say?" asked Charlie, continuing to dig politely for every possible detail.

"He was pretty thick," said Wesley. "He sure was heavier than me. Like maybe he played on the little monster football team or something. I guess his shoulders were pretty wide, too."

"That's great, Wesley," said Charlie. "What else can you remember?"

Holding a small race car, the boy ran the car up and down his leg.

Clearly focusing rather intently on his memories now, Wesley said, "Well, I sort of walked over to the screen door to get a better look at the guy. He kind of looked at me like he was curious about me, just like I was kind of curious about him. When I got close to him, he looked me right in the eyes, then he real quick looked down at the fire truck I was holding. He really, really seemed to like that truck."

"So you didn't feel scared of the creature?" asked Charlie.

"Oh no," said Wesley with a quick and unequivocal reply. "This guy just seemed real curious."

Wesley's account continued. "I held the truck up on my side of the screen, and the monster put one of his hands up on the other side...like he was trying to touch the truck through the screen. So I guess we were only a couple of inches apart then. That's when I noticed that he stunk pretty bad. So I zoomed the truck across the screen a few times, and the monster ran his hand right along with what I was doing. I never seen anything like that."

"Then I asked him a couple of questions, like what his name was and where he was from, but he didn't say anything back. I don't know if he can talk at all. Do many monsters talk?" asked Wesley, looking over at Charlie.

"Well, I'd say most of them probably *don't* talk, Wesley," said Charlie. "But you were still very lucky to have met a rare creature like that."

"What's a rare?" asked Wesley.

"Yes, oh, I'm sorry," replied Charlie. "Rare means that there certainly aren't many of these creatures about. You saw something that very, very few people ever get to see."

"Oh, okay," replied Wesley. He seemed to be grasping the import of Charlie's statement.

"So, what happened next?" asked Charlie, continuing the gentle questioning.

"Well," began Wesley, "after a few minutes of both of us standing there at the door, I figured I should maybe show this guy to my parents. I held up one finger to him, kind of saying wait a minute, then I ran to the kitchen to get my mom or dad. They were both working on something in there, and I had a hard time getting anybody to come with me."

He hesitated a bit, then resumed with: "I said to them, 'Hey, there's a monster at the front door; who wants to see him?' They both looked at me like I had three or four heads," said Wesley with a mildly disappointed tone.

"My dad said to me, 'Wesley, I don't think you want to be telling tall tales.' This made me kinda' mad, so I said, 'I'm not making this up—there's a little hairy guy on our porch *right now*.'"

Wesley's mom interjected some color commentary. "Charlie, it's not like Wesley to make up stories, so when he told us about the creature, neither Sean nor I really knew how to respond. It made sense to be a little skeptical at first, particularly when the topic was a hairy monster at the front door."

Sean then joined the account dialogue. "Wesley looked pretty impatient, and he ran over and grabbed my hand. He started pulling me out of the kitchen toward the front door. I wasn't all that jazzed to go out there, but I figured the boy was pretty worked up about things, so I might as well go. He pretty much dragged me all the way to the door."

The family all looked at each other silently at this point.

"By the time we got back out there," Wesley eventually said with a slightly dejected voice, "there was nobody there."

"Tell Charlie about the next part, Wesley," instructed his mom.

"Oh, okay. I ran out the front door and started looking all around the yard for the monster. I poked my head in the bushes by the front of the house and I looked up in the trees and everyplace, but the little guy was gone."

"I went out there too," added Sean, "to help Wesley search for whatever he had seen. I scanned the yard completely and I even walked around the back of the house, but there was nothing unusual anywhere."

By this point in the extensive and detailed witness discussion, Betty had managed to attain new levels of comfort. Not following the monster narrative in any way, Betty was lying upside down on the rug, with four legs and paws pointed toward the ceiling, and Wesley was rubbing her belly affectionately. Life was again very good for this dog.

Charlie, meanwhile, was still typing furiously on his laptop, trying to keep up with documenting every detail of the boy's account.

"Wesley, you sure had the experience here," said Charlie approvingly. "Thank you so much for sharing your account with me."

"What's an account?" he asked Charlie, who again had to clarify his vocabulary.

"Oh, yes, an account is just a report or a story that you tell to someone else," he explained.

"Oh yeah, well, no problem, I guess," said Wesley. "But that wasn't all that happened."

"Oh no?" asked Charlie with some surprise.

Apparently, the family trio had discussed Wesley's encounter a number of times over the next few days. The parents asked questions of Wesley from various angles, and they noted that Wesley's rather detailed responses were entirely consistent each time. They were becoming more and more convinced that the boy really had seen a creature on the front porch, even though they had not seen the individual themselves. This led them to report the incident to a bigfoot researcher whom they had heard about previously.

The interesting aspects of this witness encounter did not end with the parents' report, however.

"Wesley, go ahead and tell Charlie about what you did for the creature," suggested Carole.

Still sitting in the living room with the family, Charlie perked up rapidly at the prospect of these new details.

"How 'bout if I *show* you?" asked Wesley.

Charlie looked over at the parents, who were both smiling a bit.

"Well certainly!" replied Charlie.

Having been very nearly lounging on the floor with the furry, inert beagle, Wesley quickly stood up and strode toward the front door, opened the screen door and headed toward the front yard. Charlie again reached for his laptop.

"Wait for the old people, please!" said Charlie in a sunny manner as he quickly put Betty's leash on, clumsily scuttled over and pushed open the screen door, still carrying the laptop. It was clearly time to multitask again. Everyone walked out front into the sunny Florida day under the green trees.

Wesley led the group over to one of the only areas of the front yard where there were no trees standing. Instead, there was a very low, solitary stump at this spot.

"This is where I left it for him," said Wesley, obliquely.

"Um, this here used to be a pear tree," explained Sean. "I'm pretty sure the bugs or blight got it, so I had to cut it down."

Charlie wasn't yet understanding the significance of the stumpy structure.

Finally, Wesley truncated the vagueness. "A few days after I had met this little guy, I left my firetruck on this stump as a present for him," he said somewhat proudly. "Like I said before, he *really* liked that truck."

Charlie began to feel his heart warming a bit.

He asked of Wesley, "So, what happened to the truck, young man?"

Wesley waited a moment, then dramatically answered, "I never saw it again after that day, so I'm sure he came back and took it."

Charlie was deeply impressed by the boy's generous action. He grabbed his camera and took a couple of photos of the gift stump, and of Wesley standing next to it.

"My, my," he said simply.

"We thought it was very kind of Wesley to leave one of his favorite cars for the creature," interjected Carole. "Kids don't always learn everything you try to teach them," she said, looking lovingly at Wesley, "but sharing without expecting anything in return can really be impressive when your kids do that."

"Indeed, I fully agree," echoed Charlie.

Charlie found this concluding component of Wesley's account quite touching, and its detail and sincerity also buttressed the credibility of the boy's recounting.

The parents agreed with this and reinforced that the altruistic conclusion of Wesley's tale helped further spur them to report the sighting to a bigfoot researcher.

The family, Charlie and Betty then took an aimless, leisurely stroll around the front yard. As noted previously, there wasn't any remaining physical evidence for Charlie to examine, but he enjoyed spending some idle time with the witness family amidst the lush greenery.

As the group walked back toward the house, Charlie said to Wesley, "Thank you so much for sharing your treasures with the little sasquatch," he said kindly.

Wesley stopped and gave Charlie a questioning look, and Charlie realized that the boy probably wasn't familiar with one of the alternative North American names for the creature in question.

"Sasquatch is the same as bigfoot, don't you know," he said to Wesley, hoping to clarify the nomenclature. "And a bigfoot of any age enjoys a treat once in a while. You were very kind to do that."

Wesley smiled and looked up at his approving parents.

"Um, folks, I'll be right back," said Charlie suddenly. "Wesley, will you look after Ms. Betty for a moment?"

"Sure thing," said Wesley, taking Betty's leash from Charlie and walking into the house behind his parents.

Charlie scurried without explanation toward the RV.

A couple of minutes later, he came back in through the screen door inelegantly carrying a small object behind his back.

The family eagerly looked at the eccentric but kind man as he shielded his puzzling payload.

"Amidst our tour of this great country," began Charlie, "Betty and I most recently stopped in the bayous of Louisiana. Since we often have up-close run-ins with monsters of various types, I thought I'd share with young Master Wesley here an example of the creatures with which we've become acquainted."

"Mama, I don't know what he's talkin' about," said Wesley quietly but humorously.

"Never fear, friend of monsters!" exclaimed Charlie without explanation.

He then quickly whipped out the mysterious object from behind his back. It was a green stuffed two-foot-long alligator with big, exaggerated teeth and bugged-out googly eyes. He had picked it up in a gift shop in Louisiana, and now he handed it over to Wesley.

The boy's eyes widened tremendously as he grasped the gifted green gator. It was fuzzy and fantastic.

"Oh *wow*, this guy is *great*," exclaimed Wesley as he gleefully examined his new monster friend.

The parents looked on appreciatively, clearly proud that their son's generous action had resulted in a type of pay-it-forward reciprocation.

"Thank you very much, Charlie" said Sean with obvious gratitude.

"Aw, that is *so sweet*!" exclaimed Carole, emphasizing the long e's in her short sentence.

With that, Wesley burst out of the living room and charged up the stairs, obviously to play with his new swamp treasure.

"You know, we really weren't sure how this creature encounter was going to impact Wesley," said Carole, "but being able to recount it for you, and for you to have rewarded him with the gator gift, it's really becoming pretty special. I'm sure Wesley will always remember this event and how he shared it with you."

"I appreciate you opening your home to us," said Charlie, "and allowing us to take in the full story of what happened here... during the event and afterward."

Since Wesley had ascended the stairs and was lost to his new friendship with the stuffed gator, Charlie shook hands with each of the parents and prepared to take his leave.

He put a hand up to his face and yelled up the stairs, "Bye bye, Master Wesley!"

Both of the parents reached down and gave Betty some generous scratches, and the investigators headed back to their vehicle.

Charlie fired up Motor Myrtle, and the rolling crew headed back down to the St. Mary's Cove RV park.

Later, Charlie cooked a steak sub on a roll. He took Betty for a lengthy walk around the grounds before retiring to the RV, where he finished up documenting the information gleaned from the Williams family's account that day.

The Williams report entailed the least tangible physical evidence of any of his investigations so far, but Charlie deeply appreciated how a young boy had made every effort to share in detail his experiences with the adults in his life...including the gifting for an undersized, juvenile bigfoot. This was clearly a unique experience for all concerned.

Late that night, Charlie accessed his SSDD bigfoot sighting database and mentally prepared for his trip to the next sighting location—in North Carolina.

6

FULL OF HARD KNOCKS

The travelers had quite the northward drive in front of them, needing to cross the entire south-to-north distance of the states of South Carolina and Georgia, then to south-central North Carolina. They began by picking up I-10 east, then taking I-95 north at Jacksonville. They hugged the coast going north on the hectic highway corridor for quite a few hours.

Having kept up with roaring traffic for some time, Charlie had decided to make a certain stop in South Carolina where he and Betty could take in something less

speedy and noisy. Immediately after having crossed the huge Lake Marion, just south of the town of Summerton, Motor Myrtle pulled in for a stop at the Santee National Wildlife Refuge.

This refuge is known as a major stopover point for numerous species of waterfowl including ducks, geese and wading birds, plus raptors and neo-tropical songbirds. Many other types of non-winged terrestrial creatures also reside in this preserve.

After parking Motor Myrtle at the visitors' center, Charlie took Betty on a lengthy walk across the refuge grounds and trails. Crisscrossing the marshy, wooded expanse, they spotted countless birds fluttering and feeding, and Betty woofed at most of them.

This stop, replete with plenty of bipedal and quadrupedal exercise, proved to be a relaxing respite from the churn of the highway.

Later, continuing north, Motor Myrtle ducked off I-95 and headed west to the town of Sumter, where Charlie hoped to grab some yummy nutrients and stop for the night. They landed at a bistro in town where Charlie enjoyed shrimp and grits along with fried green tomatoes. Betty of course was thrilled when Charlie returned to Motor Myrtle with the shrimp and grits beagle bag.

They stayed the night at a nearby RV park in Sumter.

The next morning, after procuring an early breakfast from a local grille including a heavily loaded omelet for Charlie and ample eggy leftovers for the young lady of the rig, Charlie headed back toward I-95 north in the direction of North Carolina.

Eventually they took roads north toward the town of Mount Gilead. This town is at the lower end of the Uwharrie National Forest—a region known for many bigfoot sightings across time.

Prior to this late September day, Charlie had arranged to meet the next witness, Kevin Townsend, at a coffee shop in Mount Gilead.

Motor Myrtle pulled into the shop's parking lot, and Charlie, as usual, instructed Betty to sit tight for a while. She went into full nap mode atop one of the RV beds and didn't seem concerned about missing anything.

Walking into the venue, Charlie told the hostess that he was meeting a man here, then he looked around to see if he could spot his next witness. He didn't see any lone males in the dining area despite having walked through the table aisles.

Seeming to have struck out, he walked back up front to the hostess and said to her, "Well young lady, I can't find the man I'm supposed to meet."

She looked at him rather blankly, then looked past him. "Is this him?" she asked.

Charlie turned around to see a tall man about 60 years old with wavy graying hair striding purposefully toward him.

"Are you Charlie"" the man asked.

"Why yes, I'm Charlie Marlowe, and I presume you're Kevin Townsend," he said.

"That's right. It's nice to meet you," said Kevin. The two men shook hands. "And I'm sorry for the delay; I needed to see a man about a horse," explained Kevin, regarding his advance from the restroom region.

"Sometimes, horses take priority," opined Charlie.

Kevin laughed. He was a rather thin man, easily more than six feet tall, wearing running shorts (even at this autumnal date), tennis shoes and an orange, collared polo shirt with short sleeves. Charlie perceived that Kevin had a somewhat athletic stature despite his advancing years.

"I've got a table for us over this way," he said, pointing to a small, round table with barstools next to a low couch where patrons could lounge and indulge in caffeine and pastries in the quaint, fragrant, slightly dark coffee shop.

"Very good, Kevin," said Charlie as he followed Kevin over to the table and sat down on one of the stools. Getting settled, Charlie asked, "Do you mind if I deploy my notetaking gear?"

Kevin watched Charlie pull the laptop out of his bag and prepare to open it on the table. "Sure, that's fine." Country music played over the coffee shop sound system. There wasn't much of a crowd in the shop at this hour.

"Would you like a beverage?" Kevin asked, and Charlie replied in the affirmative regarding a basic, unadorned cup of coffee. "Okay then, I'll order," Kevin added.

With that he walked up to the front counter to order coffees and some snacks. Meanwhile Charlie got his laptop fully fired up as he prepared to document Kevin's account.

Several minutes later Kevin returned with two coffees in paper cups and several warm cheese danish treats.

"Well isn't that lovely?" exclaimed Charlie. "Thank you very much Kevin, and how much do I owe you?

"It's on the house," said Kevin. "I'm likely to dump a major heap of information on you, and you might benefit from some advance sustenance."

"That's much appreciated," said Charlie. "So, what sorts of things have you encountered in the bigfoot realm here?" he asked as he bit into the pastry and took his first swig of steaming hot coffee, very nearly burning his mouth.

Kevin sat still and silent for some time, then said, "I've run into a lot of things that aren't really easy to explain. I've been frightened, perplexed, astounded, mystified, and probably a bunch of other things."

"So, please describe the locations and what you've observed," said Charlie, setting down his coffee cup and preparing to type.

Charlie's introductory instruction launched Kevin into the extensive retelling of a host of incidents that occurred in close temporal and physical proximity. Given the man's rather precise use of vocabulary and clarity of recollection, Charlie quickly recognized that Kevin was quite a capable witness.

Setting out on his account, Kevin said, "I experienced a number of rather unusual incidents while visiting and staying with an old retired friend of mine in the area, Scott Dunham, who owns a vacation cabin on the fringes of the Uwharrie National Forest. (I used to work with Scott in the defense industry.) Scott's house is in a group of homes up in the high-elevation woods on steep slopes, with everything accessed by gravel roads. It's not too far away from town down here," he added, "but it's a change in elevation."

He went on. "Anyway, on the first day, I was up there at Scott's little mountain cabin. It sits atop a well-wooded bluff, where the elevation behind the house drops sharply. We spent a nice afternoon just hanging out, strolling around the property a bit, and downing a few beers as we talked about sports and family, and rehashed some crusty old work tales. We had a leisurely dinner and then sat out on the back porch to watch the sun go down and listen to the sounds of the woods. We were just sitting there minding our own business as darkness fell."

"We had been outside probably less than a half an hour," he resumed, "when we heard some loud wood knocks coming from the trees way down the hill from the house. There was kind of a thump on a tree that came from one direction, then another sharp wood crack about five or ten seconds later—an answering sound, it seemed—that came from a *different* direction."

Kevin continued with his account, saying, "The dual knock sounds were repeated every couple of minutes for—I guess—about 15 minutes or so, and it sounded as if the second of the knocks was actually changing positions slightly."

"So I decided to ask Scott, 'Are there folks out in these woods at night who might be making these noises?'"

Scott apparently didn't hesitate replying at all. "Oh no," he began, "Almost everyone up here is retired, and being older, they don't traipse around the forest making a ruckus after dark. I'm sure of it. The sounds we're hearing aren't people."

Scott's resolute response felt bewildering to Kevin, since the sounds were so clear and their bidirectional orientation so unmistakable. What sorts of individuals could produce such distinctive sounds, he thought?

"Well geez, if it's not people, then what is it?!" Kevin asked of Scott, continuing to be slightly incredulous about the unusual, literally striking sounds they'd heard.

Scott apparently smiled and looked down for a few moments before saying, "Folks say there are some big forest dwellers around here who kind of march to the beat of their own drummer." As Kevin gave him yet another highly bewildered look, Scott clarified, "It might just be bigfoot, my friend."

"Wow," exclaimed Kevin, "I didn't know you were allowed to have so much...fun...in retirement."

Scott responded with a knowing laugh.

Without much delay, Kevin walked down to a tall, abundantly stocked woodpile next to the back deck. He grabbed a sturdy length of cut log and whacked it a single time against the trunk of a tall, nearby hardwood tree.

Within eight or ten seconds, a knock resonated from out in the dark forest, seemingly in answer to the sound Kevin had generated.

"Wow, did you get that?!" he asked his friend Scott (who was above him on the deck) with an insistent whisper.

"Yup, that's how we roll around here," replied Scott from above, equally quietly and impishly.

Still holding the length of log, Kevin struck the nearby tree twice this time, resulting in two loud wooden thwacks.

Another ten or so seconds passed. Soon, two knocks came from an opposing direction in the woods.

"Man, that's *incredible*," said Kevin to Scott, who was still thoroughly relaxing on the porch and enjoying his beverage.

"You just never know who you're going to meet out here," said Scott.

This time, Kevin hit the tree three times with loud knocks. However, there was no equivalent reply.

He waited several minutes and executed another triple knock aftershock. Once again, there was no reply. The forest conversation having apparently ended, Kevin reluctantly returned the log to the pile and rejoined Scott on a deck chair upon the back porch.

"Well, that was pretty amazing," said Kevin to Scott summarily.

They stayed on the back deck for a while, then retired inside for the remainder of the night.

Kevin went to bed that night in a heightened state of excitement over having communicated with something large, responsive, and possibly intelligent—in the woods. Sleep did not come quickly that night, as it often doesn't when visiting a new, unfamiliar environment.

"Late the next morning," continued Kevin, "I went for a run on the looping, hilly roads that snake through the development. I noticed that I was struggling to breathe a bit in the thinner air at an elevation that I wasn't terribly accustomed to, but the beauty of the setting made the labored breathing worth it."

"I'd been jogging for about ten minutes when I started to get the strange feeling that I was being watched. There wasn't anything that I could put my finger on," he explained, "but it just felt like I wasn't alone as I passed through certain heavily wooded areas where there weren't any houses around."

"I stopped to rest and look around momentarily in one of the undeveloped areas, and on a fairly steep dirt bank next to the road, I spotted a line of very large, human-like footprints leading up the hill in the dirt. The tracks were quite clear."

"As I followed the tracks up the dirt grade with my sight, I could see that, after reaching the top of the hill, they led to what looked like a game trail, or narrow clearing of weeds, continuing into the woods."

"Ah yes," replied Charlie, "I've followed many a game trail into the uncertain oblivion of the forest."

Kevin continued, "Anyway, back down on the dirt hill, I moved in and looked more closely at the individual tracks. The heel portion of the prints sunk pretty far down into the dirt...maybe three or four inches in depth. I also could see very clear toe impressions at the top of each footprint. So, this wasn't someone wearing hiking boots. And the overall prints were long...much longer than a human's footprint. I was pretty amazed by what I was seeing, and it got me thinking again about the possible presence of a bigfoot in the area."

Charlie again gently interrupted the witness monologue, asking, "Kevin, do you think you could show me the spot in the mountains where you observed the creature's tracks?"

"Well sure, I don't think they'd be *too* hard to find at this point," replied Kevin, essentially thinking out loud. Looking up toward the ceiling, he added, "I can clearly remember the part of the road where I stopped during my run, and the game trail visible at the top of the grade should be a helpful marker."

"Perhaps we could scoot past that area after our talk today," said Charlie, "but by all means, please continue with your description, Kevin."

"Uh, so," resumed Kevin, hesitating for a few moments to regain the chronology of his narrative, "that was really about it with regard to the tracks I found and my run through the mountain roads. However, this story isn't *nearly* done," he said to Charlie with a slight smile.

"It really picks up again that same night, after dinner," began Kevin. "Scott really wanted to watch a ballgame on TV, but I was still pretty intrigued by the nighttime goings on at this cabin, so I went out back on the deck by myself just to listen."

"I sat there doing nothing for nearly a half an hour, and thinking that perhaps I should have stayed inside and bet with Scott on the game's outcome. However, the knocks started again, coming from the direction of the first knock the night before."

"I knocked back by hitting another small log against a tree, and I got some 'replies' to my knocks" he added. "But then, after a short period of silence, a long, eerie howl started up from the opposite direction of where tonight's knocks were coming from. It was a very strange sound—unlike any animal I've heard before—and it was pretty unsettling. It just pierced the whole area and sort of silenced everything else."

Kevin reported that the plaintive howls reoccurred approximately every couple of minutes or so for about ten, or perhaps 15, minutes.

"Eventually I went back into Scott's great room and forcibly pulled him away from the TV and outside for a few minutes. Fortunately, he was able to hear the last couple of howls that the creature or creatures produced."

"Scott said to me, 'Wow, I suppose our forest friends have quite a bit to say tonight. Now can I get back to the game?'"

"The howls stopped at that point and I was ready to head back inside for the night," said Kevin. "Fortunately for Scott, the Tar Heels beat Virginia Tech in a nighttime gridiron slugfest."

"Later that night I sunk into bed and resumed reading one of the books I'd brought along. I was still a little bit amped at having heard the creature sounds, but I was getting pretty relaxed reading in bed and I was anticipating a decent night's sleep. After an hour or so of reading I clicked off the light and fell asleep pretty quickly, I believe. It's very quiet way out here in the woods at night."

Kevin's nighttime narrative continued. "I'm not really sure how long I'd been asleep, but I sort of got jolted awake by what sounded like someone walking on the roof of the cabin…right over my head! For the life of me I couldn't figure out who would be up on my friend's cabin roof in the middle of the night. It made no sense at all. I just lay there listening to this…something… crossing the roofline with heavy steps."

"Right after that," continued Kevin, "I heard some thumps or knocks or something making impact with the cabin roof above the *opposite* side of my room, like over the closet area, though it didn't sound like someone walking this time. It was more thump-like and irregular."

"So, here I am again listening to two sets of mysterious sounds very close by," said Kevin. "I could not figure out what was going on, and in the middle of a very dark night, you can probably imagine how unnerving it was."

Kevin continued. "The footsteps and thumps soon quieted down and stopped. I lay there for a long time thinking about what I'd heard and wondering what could have generated the sounds, but eventually I fell back asleep."

"Then, after another indeterminate time," he said, "I was *again* jolted awake—this time by someone pounding on the walls of the room from outside! The impacts—which sounded like heavy fists—were just shocking. The walls right next to me were actually shaking. The noise was incredibly loud and in my freshly-awakened stupor, I figured that perhaps someone must have been breaking into my room. I thought maybe I should go yell for Scott to see if he had a gun or something, but to begin with I just sat up in bed and clicked on the room's overhead light to instigate some change."

"Given how incredibly loud the wall banging was, I started to think that this must be a bigfoot making these sounds since the prior wood knocks and howls had been pretty close by, and Scott had pretty resolutely ruled out human origin."

Kevin's attempts to figure out the puzzle continued. "So I tried turning out the light now in hopes of being able to spot something outside. I crept over to the window and strained as my eyes got used to the full darkness again, but I couldn't see anyone or anything out there. I got back in bed for a few minutes, then a sound like hands slapping the walls started. I couldn't believe it! The noises were sort of higher in pitch than the prior fist pounding…more like cracks and slaps than thuds. But they were still just as shocking to hear in the middle of the night. So by this point I'm thinking, 'Holy crap, what have I gotten myself into?'"

"Like some of the other sounds," said Kevin, "they seemed to come from opposing sides of my room...like one creature in front of the house and one on the side or back of the house, perhaps. Then I decided to unlock and open the window, trying to hear something, and at that point I did hear some big footsteps receding through the leaf litter in the yard. I thought again about waking Scott, but decided to look into this on my own."

He added, "I quickly walked down the hall, went through the kitchen and unlocked the sliding glass door to the back deck. I stepped outside on full alert—completely ready to retreat back inside if these huge things showed up. As I stood there, I heard at least one figure walking away from the property into the deeper woods. Although the sound gave me the creeps, the prospect of the night monsters withdrawing into the woods was suddenly kind of comforting."

"As I listened to the crunching footsteps get quieter and quieter," said Kevin, "I realized for the first time that I was shaking all over. I hurried back inside and locked that glass door behind me real fast. Then I hit up Scott's liquor cabinet for something strong." Charlie giggled at this detail.

"In time I got back in bed and tried to settle down and get back to sleep, but *man*, it took a long time. The next morning I told Scott about what had happened (he sleeps like a non-knocking log), and all he said was, 'Never a dull moment out here, my friend.' His level of empathy wasn't exactly impressive."

Still sitting across from Kevin in the coffee shop, Charlie strove to take in everything that Kevin had shared with him. He had been typing like a fiend throughout Kevin's narrative, and the two men had gone through several cups of coffee.

"That's just an amazing story of your time in the mountains, Kevin," said Charlie. "You very nearly got up close and personal with those noisy creatures."

"Yes, and having some flimsy wallboard and wood between me and those animals was something I don't want to do again soon," replied Kevin.

"Well, speaking of soon," said Charlie, "might you be ready to show me the location where you observed the bigfoot trackway?"

Kevin considered the question momentarily and replied, "Yeah, as long as we're doing this during the day, it's okay. At night, I don't really want to be out there."

Kevin kindly paid the coffee shop bill as Charlie gathered up his gear and got ready for the next short investigative trek.

Fortunately, there were some cheese danish shards remaining after Charlie and Kevin's talk, and Charlie stopped outside at the RV to give them to an appreciative Betty as he walked her around the parking lot to relieve herself. Kevin got a laugh out of the obvious beagle spoilage.

Standing near the RV before heading to his car, Kevin said, "You know, you can bring your dog along if you'd like. I have a shepherd/husky mix at home named Kiana, and she would in no way want to miss an outing like this if she had a chance."

"Well that's very kind of you, Kevin. Betty will serve as splendid company to us as we head up that hill." The two humans and the dog got into Kevin's sedan and headed toward additional evidence.

The drive out of the small town of Mt. Gilead into the hilly forest of the Uwharrie was short. Sitting in the passenger seat, Charlie observed the elevation changing quickly, and soon the group was on the winding dirt-and-gravel roads of the isolated development where Kevin had had his experiences.

While driving, Kevin began scanning the terrain very closely, in addition to slowing down as the car entered one of the zones where no houses existed. He was looking up the hill to his right when he seemed to spot something that caught his eye.

"Here we are," he said to Charlie and Betty. Pointing, he said, "That dirt rise there contains the tracks." Charlie could actually see the outlines of some footprints from the car. In the back seat, Betty had her paws up on the door and her snout out the partially open window. She was observing everything out the window very closely.

"Great," said Charlie, simply.

Kevin pulled the car slightly off the narrow road and stopped, with two tires on the road and two in the weeds. Everyone got out. Charlie, of course, lugged his backpack full of investigative gear, plus another bag with as-yet-uncertain contents. Charlie asked Kevin if he would temporarily handle Betty on leash, and Kevin agreed without hesitation.

"It's right over here," said Kevin. "We'll see how kind the weather has been to the tracks."

Charlie eagerly followed Kevin toward the target of the investigation—massive monster footprints—at least he hoped.

Kevin walked to the bottom of the small dirt rise and stopped to look closely at the steep soil hill.

"They still look great," he said to Charlie, who moved right in next to Kevin to observe the evidence.

There, right in front of him, were three or four gigantic footprints imbedded in the dirt, leading to the top of the hill where they disappeared into brush, seemingly. Behind that brush was a huge stand of deciduous trees that formed an imposing green wall.

"Oh my, these tracks are *wonderful*," exclaimed Charlie.

Betty was slightly indifferent to the find, straining at the leash in an effort to run off into the woods for adventures. A fellow dog owner, Kevin knew how to wrangle Betty, fortunately.

As usual, Charlie dove into his backpack to extract his tools. He pulled out his tape measure and laptop, but he also grabbed some other items out of the extra bag.

Charlie went up to the first of the prints, about four feet up from the level of the road, and unspooled his tape measure parallel to the first print.

"Seventeen and 5/8ths inches," he said proudly to the others.

"Uh, that's a really big forest fellow," said Kevin.

Charlie began snapping pictures. After taking several, he moved on to the next print which was another three or four feet up the dirt hill. He laid the tape measure down next to it.

"This one is *outstanding*!" he cried. "It's worthy of casting, basically."

Kevin didn't immediately grasp what Charlie was talking about, but he soon figured it out.

Charlie took a few pictures of the second print, then retreated to his extra bag. He pulled out a plaster of paris sack, a jug of water and a large plastic bowl. He dumped the ingredients into the bowl and began stirring up whatever snow-white slimy concoction this was.

As Kevin observed Charlie's stirring process, he saw the consistency of the white goop thicken up rapidly. Charlie carried the bowl over to the second print and dumped the contents carefully into the large impression. The plaster mostly filled the print. Charlie seemed pleased.

"This is one of the better prints I've seen in my travels," he said, "and hopefully the track cast will come out well."

With that, he backed up to once again examine the dirt hill in front of him, leading into the deeper forest.

Charlie counted three bigfoot tracks in all. He somewhat clumsily climbed the dirt hill parallel to the tracks so he could get a different perspective on the find. He let his eyes follow the game trail that connected the bigfoot tracks with the green forest wall. This was an excellent evidence discovery. Charlie took more pictures of the surroundings.

The two men, with Betty in tow, walked around the area together for some time, talking more about Kevin's experience with the creatures he'd heard.

After 35 or 40 minutes, Charlie returned to the casted track and began ever-so-carefully pulling it up from the dirt. It came out in one piece and seemingly in sound condition. Charlie was thrilled as he gently knocked the dirt off the bottom of the track, revealing the details of foot shape and toe impressions. Looking very closely at what he had cast, Charlie observed that the track had the characteristic long, straight heel, the five-toed array, and the mid-tarsal break or flexible foot that's common in bigfoot morphology.

"Thank you so much for showing us this area, Kevin!" said Charlie with obvious appreciation. "This sort of evidence is positively *invaluable.*"

Kevin opened the trunk of his car, where Charlie very gingerly set down the track cast and his equipment satchels.

"All good!" exclaimed Charlie.

Betty was ready to get back to Motor Myrtle for dinner.

The trio headed back down the hill, and Kevin dropped Charlie and Betty off at the coffee shop lot. Charlie again thanked Kevin heartily for his time and information, and Kevin said his goodbyes to the investigator and his four-legged traveling companion.

With the day elapsing, Motor Myrtle headed to one of the many family camping areas in Mt. Gilead, Norwood Campground. Charlie checked in and drove back to his campsite amidst the tall hardwoods, hooking up his 50-amp power cable, water and sewer connections. Later, heading out for a walk, Charlie and Betty visited a little pond on the campground site, then headed across the street to Lake Tillery, where the duo enjoyed quite a bit of quiet, relaxing time walking along the bank of the expansive lake.

Charlie cooked hotdogs that night, and into the evening, Charlie (as usual) organized and edited the witness notes he had taken that day. Charlie hit the bed pretty early that night, and of course, Betty snuggled right up against his legs for maximum comfort. Charlie fell asleep thinking about his now distant wife, Francesca, back in Santa Fe. He wondered how she was doing. Overall, Charlie and Betty had a pleasant though brief stay at Norwood.

The next day, Charlie made an unglamorous cereal/kibble breakfast for himself and Betty, and prepared for the next leg of the journey. It would not be a particularly quick jaunt to their next destination.

The Motor Myrtle trip began with a lazy drive through the Uwharrie, then continued up to Greensboro, North Carolina where they took BR-29 north into Virginia. Heading west, they eventually hit I-81, and they stayed on that all the way through Virginia along the Appalachian Mountains, through western Maryland and into Pennsylvania. This segment of the drive took more than seven hours, with a lunch stop near Richmond and a brush with the weighty burg of Washington, D.C.

7

SWAMP SQUATCH OF THE ALLEGHENY

Charlie planned this leg of the trip to encompass a novel component: a visit with one of his relatives. He had a sister named Evangeline who lived in the town of Hanover, Pennsylvania. He hadn't seen her in a few years and wanted to take this rare East Coast opportunity to revel in some family time.

So, rolling into Pennsylvania on I-81, Motor Myrtle took Rt. 116 west to Hanover, a quaint historic and industrial town near the famous Civil War battle town of Gettysburg.

Motor Myrtle rolled up to Charlie's sister's address within the city limits and stopped in the street.

Charlie scurried up to the house where Evangeline met him, hugged him, and told him he could pull the RV into her driveway.

Differing from most of the other stops on this multistate monster march, downtown Hanover consisted of lots of old townhouses and businesses along a tree-lined, historic urban streetscape that didn't look altogether different from Civil War times—except that there were a few more vaping and cellphone shops now. The roads were narrow, busy and loud, but Charlie enjoyed the change of pace this environment provided.

After undergoing a slightly agonizing process in reverse gear—getting Myrtle squeezed into the narrow driveway right next to Evangeline's aged, gray-shingled, two-story home—Charlie headed inside to introduce Betty and get reacquainted with his older sister.

Evangeline was a slight woman with a friendly face, sporting grayish straight hair pulled back tightly into a ponytail. She wore nerdy glasses along with a floral print white top, a denim vest and a dark skirt. She looked quite smart and together.

As Charlie came up the front steps to the covered porch in front of the house, he made Betty the center of attention.

"Angie, I'd like you to meet my copilot and co-conspirator, Betty," he said cheerfully.

"Oh, isn't she *precious*?!" exclaimed Evangeline, kneeling down to pet the little beagle and in turn receive effusive facial licks. "I've heard about her but haven't yet met her. Um, I've got two cats inside, but it's likely that—in their panic—they'll cloister themselves beneath furniture or in closets for the duration."

"Not to worry, my beloved sibling," said Charlie with an overly dramatic, stentorian tone—his arm now around Evangeline. "Betty hasn't consumed a feline in over ten hours now," he said without a shred of honesty. Evangeline giggled at her little brother's customary foray into wordy, oddball flights of phonetic fancy.

"Oh, I've sure missed you, you know," she said to him kindly, giving him an extra squeeze around his ample midsection.

"I've missed you right back," Charlie replied.

The two humans and dog headed inside the house and got themselves settled. Charlie visited the bathroom facilities while Betty sniffed every single thing in the home within nasal reach. Evangeline was prepping some items for a later chicken dinner. Betty, supervising Evangeline closely in the kitchen, received some welcome leavings.

Before long, Betty, Charlie and Evangeline were deeply comfortable sitting on Evangeline's sunny back porch. An old alley full of garages, other outbuildings and trash cans ran behind Evangeline's property and separated it from the properties behind. The smells of roofing tar and unidentifiable factory odors drifted through the neighborhood.

Charlie selected a wide porch swing for seating, and Betty jumped up into Evangeline's lap on a deck chair. The group visited and caught up on myriad topics of interest throughout the afternoon and into the cool early October evening.

As hunger began to gnaw a bit at the travelers, Charlie asked Evangeline about something of which he was aware in the area.

"And hey, Angie, can I take Betty on a tour through the Utz plant?" he asked out of the blue. The large, multi-site chip and snack plant was one of the most prominent old businesses in the area, and Charlie's thoughts had drifted toward some of his favorite Utz comestibles such as crab chips, cheese balls and Carolina barbeque chips.

"You're welcome to drive over there," began Evangeline, "but Betty's likely going to have to sit that one out. I fear she'd go on a snack attack and clean out the factory."

Charlie laughed as he considered this scenario, and replied, "Yeah, you're probably right."

"Since it's obvious that you're getting hungry, why don't I head back in and finish up making dinner?"

Charlie was instantly on board with that proposition. "Far be it from me to detain you," he said.

Everyone headed back inside at this point.

Evangeline was kind enough to prepare a baked chicken dinner topped with cream cheese for the travelers, complete with sides of cheesy mashed potatoes, green beans and asparagus, roasted tomatoes, and apple pie for dessert. Charlie was extremely appreciative of the lovely meal his sister prepared, and Betty clearly loved the chicken scraps that came her way during and after dinner. As usual, this dog was living pretty well.

Later, back out on the porch, Charlie and Evangeline continued to talk and catch up on family and world issues over the course of the next several hours. At one point Evangeline inquired about the state of Charlie's retirement.

"Are you enjoying yourself in retirement so far?"

Charlie didn't hesitate to respond. "Oh yes," he said. "I got off to a rather slow start, but this perambulation of the nation has fully freed me from the bonds of career captivity. We've seen some amazing things on this trip, and we're nowhere near done. I do miss Francesca a bit, though," he admitted. "Okay, a lot," he quickly tacked on.

"Yes, it's tough to be alone—Betty excepted, of course," said Evangeline.

"And how are you getting along without Bob?" asked Charlie, referring to Evangeline's late husband of more than 30 years who had passed away a couple of years prior. Charlie had liked Bob quite a bit.

"I'll admit this isn't the way I wanted my later years to unfold," said Evangeline somewhat sadly, "but I'm trying to hang in there." Brightening somewhat, she added, "My cats Mr. Snuffles and Rufus do keep me guessing."

"Oh, I simply *must* meet any cat named Mr. Snuffles," said Charlie with exaggerated insistence. (Evangeline later obliged with said introduction, leading Charlie upstairs to an essentially dedicated cat room containing climbing towers, food tables, water bowls and kitty latrines.)

As the sun started to go down, the group got up to head inside. First, Charlie took Betty for a walk around the back yard.

Evangeline had an extra room in which the traveling duo could stay overnight, so they took some time to ready their sleeping and toiletry arrangements.

That night, Charlie got a good night's sleep in an actual bed. Betty slept at his feet, and they enjoyed the rare comforts of indoor slumber.

The next morning, Charlie and Evangeline together prepared a hearty breakfast of scrambled eggs, bacon and toast, with some fruit on the side. Betty didn't turn down any of the bacon that came her way.

After breakfast and packing up, Charlie and Betty headed out the front door.

"Take care, my brotherly world traveler," sang Evangeline to Charlie as he prepared for his departure from southern Pennsylvania. She gave him a big, extended hug.

"And hey," said Charlie, "Maybe one of these years you'll accompany me into the forest in search of monsters."

Evangeline was quiet for a few moments, and replied, "I've got two monsters here in this house, and I've got my hands full keeping them civilized. But thanks very much." As the travelers were climbing up into their rig, Evangeline shouted, "And give my best to Francesca!"

With that, Charlie prepared Motor Myrtle for a four-hour drive largely due north. The rig wheeled out toward Rt. 94 north, with Evangeline waving goodbye from her front porch. At the wheel, waving back, Charlie shed a tear or two in recognition of the fact that seeing distant loved ones was an infrequent occurrence at best.

Motor Myrtle's destination was the Allegheny National Forest, a huge wilderness, wildlife and recreational area spanning four counties in northwestern Pennsylvania. A witness had contacted the SSDD with a report of a terrifying encounter with a sasquatch in this deeply wooded area.

Myrtle's route was basically a north by northwest trek through Pennsylvania. Much of the travel time occurred on US-322 west and the major Pennsylvania Route I-80 before transitioning to smaller rural roads that led directly north into the town of Marienville. This town lies at the southern border of the Allegheny National Forest.

Late in the day, Motor Myrtle rolled into a cabin-and-campground park called Forest Ridge. The RV sites were expansive and tucked cozily between tall green trees that surrounded everything. As usual, after checking in and hooking up, Charlie took Betty for a lengthy walk around the wooded grounds, which Betty enjoyed. The park had ample playgrounds and ballfields, and Betty enjoyed watching the kids scurrying about amidst their playtime.

An SSDD member based in Pennsylvania named Steve Troves had previously contacted Charlie with the name and location of one of a group of witnesses to an unusual bigfoot encounter that occurred on the edge of the huge, 500,000+ acre national forest.

The witness, Lauren Wetzel, had apparently been out trail walking with some friends one evening when the group ran into a sasquatch-type creature. She had reported the sighting to the SSDD information hub.

Charlie had arranged to meet Lauren late on the following morning at a barbecue eatery in town along Rt. 66. Arriving at the restaurant in Motor Myrtle, Charlie bid Betty a temporary adieu. Stepping out of the RV, Charlie quickly noted the fragrant smell of cooking beef. Things were looking up. Betty would be expectant.

Charlie walked into the small stone-fronted building and began scanning the seating area. A young woman stood up at one of the red faux-leather booths and walked up to him.

"I'm Lauren Wetzel," she said.

"I'm Charlie Marlowe, and it's a pleasure to meet you," said Charlie with a broad smile as he shook the young lady's hand. She had a pleasant and intelligent face. He estimated Lauren's age to be around 30 years, give or take a few ticks in either direction. She had medium-length dark hair parted in the middle, fair skin, and wore dark-rimmed glasses. She was dressed in a gray sweater with the sleeves rolled up, jeans and hiking shoes—and Charlie gathered she was no stranger to the outdoors.

"Come and join me," she said to Charlie, and he followed her to the table where she had been seated.

The two sat down together. A female server came over with a menu for Charlie; Lauren already had one.

"Are you up for some good barbecue today?" Lauren asked.

As usual Charlie didn't dither with his food-related answer. "I've been ready for some good barbecue since 1978." Lauren laughed.

"Then I think you'll like it here. The beef brisket is sensational, and you'd probably like the smoked mac and cheese too."

"Ooh, this day is improving by the minute!" said Charlie.

When the waitress returned, both of the diners ordered iced tea to accompany their early barbecue lunches. Charlie ended up taking Lauren's recommendation about ordering the brisket with a mac side, plus adding a side of coleslaw. As usual, Betty would have some delectable leftover barbecue bites brought her way after Charlie's "business" meeting.

"Please allow me to get set up here, and we'll begin," said Charlie to Lauren. He pulled the laptop out of his bag and got set for notetaking. Lauren was clearly ready to talk.

While getting set, Charlie asked, "How did you find the SSDD?"

"My friend Mark knew about it and said we should probably report the sighting," replied Lauren. "I know people often get ridiculed for reporting these things, but you can stay anonymous on the SSDD site. That appealed to me."

Her account began. "Well, one night about a month ago, two guy friends and I went out to walk along the national forest boundary. We'd done this at night a few times before and never had any problems. So it was me, plus my friends Mark and Don."

She continued. "The region I'm talking about is a deeply wooded, old-growth-type area with all kinds of animals everywhere. There's a big population of deer there, for example. The general spot was near the Buzzard Swamp Recreation Area."

"So anyway," Lauren said after taking a big drink of tea, "We had parked the car and hiked the trail only about a third of a mile in. It was about 8 at night (still in late summer) and the sky was clear, with a bright moon just starting to come up."

"Suddenly we heard a sort of high-pitched scream that lasted about five seconds. It sounded like it wasn't very far away. To me it sounded similar to the long, expressive, kind of musical cry of a coyote or something. The three of us stood stock still after the weird, creepy sound. We just stood there looking at each other and listening for 30 seconds or so to see if the sound occurred again. It didn't. We talked for a minute about what the sound could have been. Without having any really good ideas, we resumed our hike."

"Further along the trail a little bit, we came to a clearing that had a small, marshy swamp surrounded by a stand of really big trees. The sun was going down at this point, but we could still see the wake of some beavers and ducks swimming in the swamp. The sunset over this spot was quite pretty. There were the typical sounds of late-season insects and frogs all around."

"Mark and Don and I all stopped together in the clearing to talk about how nice this spot was. We'd been there about a minute when an enormously angry, powerful roar exploded from—it seemed like—right in the middle of the swamp! It was incredibly loud and threatening, but at first we couldn't see what kind of creature might have made the sound. There were cattails and old wood chunks or something at some edges of the water and you couldn't see anything real clearly at this hour."

"Anyway, the roar lasted about eight to ten seconds—much longer than the first cry we had heard. The difference this time was that the sound seemed to be *much* closer to us. It was very deep this time. It was like a full-body punch that made my body, um, vibrate...I guess. I'd estimate it at approximately only 75 to 100 feet away. We all froze dead in our tracks with fear. None of us could speak at all. I had no idea what to expect at this point. This noise was unlike anything I'd ever heard, and it seemed to be right here in the swamp. I was completely terrified."

"After a few quiet moments, I could see a huge dark creature beginning to churn through the water right toward us. It was incredible! The sun was going down in the west sort of behind the swamp, so I couldn't see any facial features on this thing as it moved toward us. That was very scary and spooky. All I could see was this gigantic, dark, human-shaped figure. It was definitely walking on two legs and swinging really heavy arms as it walked...or ran...or whatever... through the water. Its torso was massive. It was unbelievable, really."

"As it churned toward us it actually made violent waves that shot out in all directions across the water. The beavers and ducks probably didn't appreciate that too much. I simply couldn't believe how fast it was coming toward us even though the thing was waist-deep in water, gunk and cattails."

"My goodness," said Charlie in genuine solidarity with the witness of such an astounding, threatening sight.

"So, to give you more of a specific idea of what we saw, if I can," resumed Lauren, "I'd say that the width of its shoulders was at least three and a half feet, up to maybe four feet wide. It didn't look like it had much of a neck; its head seemed almost plopped down on the big, wide shoulders. Long, dark, dripping hair trailed off the arms and the midsection. Don, Mark and I talked about it later and agreed that the creature must have been at least 400 pounds."

Charlie asked Lauren how close the creature got to the group as it charged through the swamp.

"Well," she began, "this huge thing kept coming, and by the time it got about twenty feet or so off our side of the shore, we'd all had enough. Don snapped us out of our stupor, saying, 'Let's get out of here!' Each of us instantly turned and started running full speed back the way we'd come in on the trail. When we'd run a couple hundred feet on the trail toward our car, I turned around once to see if this thing was chasing us. I *really* hoped that it wasn't. I'll never forget what I saw. Again, even though it was getting dark, you could still see a little bit."

"This massively tall man/creature was just standing on the bank of the pond right where we'd been a few seconds before. It was staring in our direction and it sort of looked like it had two fists clenched down at its sides...at about the level of its knees...so I knew without any doubt that it wasn't a man. Fortunately it didn't pursue us from that point. We'd have been three little swamp snacks if it had," said Lauren ruefully.

"You're very fortunate, it sounds like," said Charlie, again empathically.

"You bet. I *really* don't think that thing wanted us to be there. So, we finished our sprint back to the car, and we drove to a different trailhead parking area a few miles away, for safety, and to try and figure out what to do. We sat there, with me sitting on the hood of the car and the guys walking around nervously, talking about this amazing thing that had just happened. We agreed that this was no human prank that we'd seen, given the obvious massiveness of this creature and the power with which it muscled its way *so* fast through the water. It also let loose that monstrous roar that no person could have produced."

"The other reason we ruled out a human prank was that we were pretty much off the beaten path on a remote trail at sundown, and there is no reason at all that someone would have dressed as a huge animal and burst out of a swamp to pursue us just as we got there. The human angle didn't add up at all," surmised Lauren, "so that's pretty much why we reported the sighting."

"I concur with you entirely, Ms. Wetzel, and I'm glad you did report," said Charlie, simply.

He attended to furiously typing notes for a few moments, then he seemed to have a thought, and stopped what he was doing.

"Could you show me the site of your bigfoot encounter?" he asked Lauren.

She agreed rather readily.

"And also, I have a girlfriend I'd like to bring along. She's a big fan of monster mysteries," Charlie said.

Lauren looked back at him with a perplexed face, but eventually replied, "Oh, okay."

Charlie and Lauren had finished their meal and Charlie packed up. Of course, Charlie didn't finish his *entire* meal, and made sure that he got a doggy bag that included some leftover beef brisket and a spot of smoked mac and cheese...for his "girlfriend."

Out in the parking lot, Charlie took Betty out on leash and introduced her to Lauren.

"You've got good taste in women," said Lauren, riffing on Charlie's relationship theme.

"This little girl keeps me in line," said Charlie, "and she eats pretty well too."

"I can see that," said Lauren after watching Betty wolf down the meat and mac.

With Charlie and Betty directing Motor Myrtle, and Lauren in her little blue Kia, they headed for the southern portion of the national forest. Lauren drove in front in order to guide the RV passengers toward the right spot. The group pulled off the road near a trailhead.

With Betty jogging freely this time (sans leash), the trio walked a bit into the woods until the trees started to thin out somewhat. Soon Lauren led them to a lonely swamp area just off the trail where the monster encounter apparently happened.

Although the temperature was not terribly warm on this October day, the atmosphere around the water was still quite buggy. Lauren showed Charlie where the group of three friends had stood when they first saw the sasquatch advancing, the creature's general path through the water, and where the group last saw the creature standing as they retreated—at the very spot where Charlie, Betty and Lauren stood now.

Charlie bent down and very closely examined the muddy area at the edge of the swamp, looking for possible tracks. He didn't immediately find any, since the marsh weeds grew right down into the water, covering most of the bare earth. Betty and Lauren stood together further up on the bank, watching silently.

After several minutes, the group heard a very sharp branch break echo out of the nearby wooded zone to their left. This froze everyone in position; Betty turned around and looked directly toward the trees from whence the sound emanated.

Out of the blue, Lauren said, "Um, I'm really not feeling well at this point. I don't know what to do, but something is *very* wrong," she added.

Charlie experienced a similar sensation. He looked at Lauren with some surprise and alarm, and after a few seconds, they heard the heavy rustling of leaves and branches moving toward the edge of the tree line. Some trees right at the edge began to be shaken slightly, and off-leash Betty spontaneously charged at the nearby ruckus. She got within about 50 feet of the trees.

Charlie could then discern a very tall, dark figure standing slightly back in the trees. Its shape wasn't well defined. Suddenly a medium-sized tree actually snapped off with an enormous crack, and it crashed downward and dropped very noisily out into the open field with a huge rush of air and sound—not all that far away from Betty. The woodland creature had executed a complete tree pushover! This stopped the dog's advance immediately. Charlie was particularly stunned at and fearful of this development.

He called quite insistently, "Betty, get *back* here!" He very much regretted not putting Betty on leash before they entered the woods.

The dog turned and looked toward Charlie when, at that moment, an immense, angry howl burst forth from the edge of the trees. Its power was so great that both human witnesses nearly lost their footing and dropped to the ground. The animal cry was raspy yet full of low-frequency infrasound that had a visceral impact on the bodily midsections of the witnesses.

Betty sprinted back to her master in terror, and Charlie made a fumbling effort to quickly get the dog back on her leash. Charlie blurted in an ungraceful manner, "Uh, friends, I'm afraid we need to leave *right now*."

"Yup!" cried Lauren in agreement.

Betty and Charlie turned and began running in the opposite direction with Lauren.

Between huffs of breath while running, Lauren said to Charlie, "It looks like I'm doing this *again*."

Charlie otherwise would have laughed but in general was a bit too overwhelmed and breathless to appropriately respond at this moment.

The group didn't see the obviously territorial bigfoot again, and they made it back to their vehicles safely.

Lauren jumped in and pulled her small car up next to Myrtle so that the driver's side windows of each vehicle faced each other.

"Follow me, Charlie," yelled Lauren out of the open window. "We'll meet down the road."

Charlie fired up Myrtle and followed Lauren to the next trailhead parking lot...the same location where the prior trio had regrouped after fleeing the swamp sasquatch.

Apparently out of harm's way now, Charlie parked and invited Lauren into the RV where they reviewed their just-concluded, very harrowing experience. Charlie took additional notes, offered Lauren a cold drink (she accepted) and thanked her very much for sharing her story with him—not to mention making the effort to run away from an imposing sasquatch...again.

After parting with Lauren, Charlie was feeling quite spent. While he certainly enjoyed being out in the field investigating, he wasn't sure he was in suitable physical condition to be routinely fleeing malevolent monsters in motion.

"Betty, your old master could probably use a tune-up," he said to the dog as they drove back to the Forest Ridge campground. Charlie wasn't appreciating the attendant gaggle of old-guy aches and pains currently afflicting him.

Later that day, they enjoyed some serious R&R around a campfire together, including a dinner of flame-cooked burgers and beans. Betty loved the grilled burger bites, of course. Charlie didn't give Betty any beans in order to minimize the overnight flatulence factor in the RV.

As usual after a weighty wilderness adventure, the driving duo took some time the next day to gently cruise around the huge national forest—though not near the scary swamp area from which they'd been ushered out. Charlie and Betty even got to hike on the Kinzua Sky Walk, a towering old railroad trestle turned walking trail containing a set of railroad tracks that led to the end of a stunning overlook. The track terminus had a partial glass floor through which visitors could look down 225 feet to the green forest floor below. Both Charlie and Betty found this a wonderfully scenic way to spend some leisure time on high.

The travelers spent a comfortable night back at Forest Ridge. From the RV, Charlie called Francesca to check in.

"How are you doing, sweetie?" he asked of his beloved life partner over 1,700 miles away. "I've missed you so much that I can't quite formulate the words," he added.

"That's kind, honey," began Francesca. "I've missed you too. Things are okay here, though we had a tarantula in the garage a couple of days back. I successfully encouraged him to make other living arrangements."

"A tarantula?!" exclaimed Charlie. "I'm *so* sorry I wasn't there to help you reallocate such an appalling arachnid."

"It happens," said Francesca in a tone of resignation. "I used a snow shovel to scoop him up and reacquaint him with outdoor living. Are you and Betty both well?" she asked, clearly wanting to change the subject.

Charlie thought about the question for a moment. "Well, our diets are quite robust, I must say," he replied, looking over at the slightly bulbous Betty and patting his own bulging belly, "but we continue to serve as suitable subjects of sasquatch pursuit."

"They've chased you?!" asked Francesca with obvious alarm.

"Yes," replied Charlie. "Right here in Pennsylvania, we just had a huge swamp dweller escort us unequivocally out of his zone of comfort. His manners, and his treatment of the local timber, were most ungracious," he said.

"Oh my," said Francesca in reaction. "Are you sure you want to keep doing this?"

"Yes, yes," replied Charlie reassuringly. "Although we don't always get great *physical* evidence at every investigative stop, we've still gathered ample *experiential* evidence that I'm able to add to my SSDD documentation. It's all valuable."

"Well...okay then," said Francesca, sounding as if she approved but was still concerned.

"So, good luck keeping the spiders at bay," said Charlie. "I may have to give some of those leggy fellows the old what-for when I get back," he tacked on with mock bravado.

Francesca laughed. "I'm *sure* you will, dear."

The next morning, after another rudimentary RV breakfast consisting of cinnamon frosted Pop Tarts in the toaster oven, along with milk and coffee, Charlie checked out of the RV park and headed back out to Route I-80 west toward Ohio.

8

A Sasquatch Uncorked At Salt Fork

On I-80, Charlie, Betty and Motor Myrtle continued west, then headed south toward Pittsburgh on I-79—an interstate on which they traveled for quite some time. Having later passed through Pittsburgh, they picked up US-22 west toward Cambridge, Ohio. The group's travel that day was just under four hours of driving. Their destination was Salt Fork State Park, a wilderness and recreational area renowned throughout the region (and beyond) for bigfoot encounters.

Charlie's work with recent SSDD bigfoot sighting accounts resulted in his gaining access to a newly reported incident within the state park whereby a couple on a picnic got into a scrape with at least one huge creature. This sounded just about right to Charlie.

The RV travelers arrived in Cambridge well into the afternoon and had lunch at a local eatery where Charlie got a luxurious bacon cheeseburger and a slice of chocolate peanut butter pie.

Then they made the brief drive north/northeast, pulling into Salt Fork State Park Campground to claim their reserved RV site on this October day. They would be meeting the witnesses within the park, so the nearby campground was convenient.

The park was very large and featured ample facilities for swimming, boating, golf, hiking, biking, camping, and assorted leisure luxuries accessible within the expansive, centralized lodge. The lodge also housed a conference center where outside groups held seminars on diverse topics. (One such prominent event was known as the Ohio Bigfoot Conference, which Charlie had always wanted to attend someday.)

After checking in, Charlie attended to the power, water and sewer hookups for the RV, then he took Betty for an extended walk through the trees and meadows in the late afternoon. They returned to Motor Myrtle for a light dinner.

Much later that night, with Betty loyally snuggling him, Charlie gazed out the window on his side of the RV and pondered the many stars overhead in this remote locale. He imagined Francesca as one of those blinking little wonders and longed for a reunion with her. There was more work to do first, however.

The next morning, Charlie made the very short drive in the RV to the Salt Fork Lodge and Conference Center. At the lodge's restaurant, he was supposed to meet Glenn and Linda Battson, a fairly young couple who lived not too far away from the big park. Before entering, Charlie gave Betty his usual mini speech about remaining patiently in the RV until his return.

Walking into the lobby of the airy, high-wood-ceilinged restaurant, with huge glass windows and a clear view of the woods beyond, Charlie spotted a couple sitting at the rear of the room. A female was waving to him. He assumed this was the Battson couple.

Walking up to the light wood-grained table, he cheerfully said, "If you're the Battsons, I'm Charlie Marlowe."

"Hi there, Charlie," said the female diner. "I'm Linda and this is Glenn."

"I'm glad to make your acquaintance," said Charlie, reaching across the table to shake hands with each individual as they stood up. A redhead with fair skin and a well-groomed aura, Linda looked rather sprightly in a light blue short-sleeve blouse, while Glenn, a tall man wearing a dark long-sleeve button-down shirt, didn't immediately strike Charlie as enthusiastic about the prospect of revisiting a sasquatch encounter. Charlie would look into this later.

Regardless, he sat down and set his backpack on the empty chair at the four-chair table.

"We're about to order breakfast; would you like to come along?" asked Linda.

"Why, yes of *course*," responded Charlie. "As you know, breakfast is the most important meal of the day, and I often want to savor its importance *all day long*!" he said with particular zest.

Linda laughed, and added, "Well, everything's good here for breakfast. You can't go wrong with anything on the menu."

A slightly husky, very friendly female server with blonde hair in a bun and wearing a maroon uniform arrived at the table to take orders. Linda and Glenn already had coffee, so they ordered their main courses, and Charlie ordered coffee and a French toast combination breakfast—envisioning flavorful bacon bits earmarked for Betty later on.

"Do you mind if I document our talk via laptop?" Charlie asked.

Glenn didn't look overly impressed at this proposal, but he replied, "Yeah, that's okay."

With Glenn still striking Charlie as somewhat the more taciturn spouse, Linda took the initiative to begin the couple's account of their adventure within the park.

She said, "About a month ago we were here, not too far away from this lodge, having an early evening dinner at a covered picnic shelter and table in the woods. There was a trail that led from the parking area down into the woods to the shelter."

"As we were finishing up our meal, we were pretty surprised to hear rocks starting to hit the roof over the picnic table. The rocks didn't sound too big, but we looked at each other like, 'What the hell?' since neither of us could figure out what was going on."

"Both of us turned and scanned the area in all directions to see if we could spot who might be throwing the dumb rocks," said Linda with a saucy, slightly annoyed tone. "We couldn't see anyone. That was pretty weird. After three or four minutes of occasional rock hits, and then a brief break in the action, a really big rock smashed into the roof right over us."

Glenn took over this part of the encounter description. "With such a huge, loud impact, I thought the rock might crash through the roof and land on our heads or at least on the table. We looked at each other and right away decided to scoop up what was left of our dinner and head toward the trail to get back to our car."

He continued into the next phase of the encounter. "Just as we got out of the picnic area clearing, we heard this deep, long, massive snarl behind us. The dang thing felt like a pissed off monster truck or maybe a crazy tidal wave hitting us. We both got frozen in place for a few seconds."

Linda took over the narration at this point. "We regained our senses a bit and started to jog up the trail. What began to concern both of us was that as we continued along the trail, we could now hear heavy leaf and branch crunching as something seemed to be walking parallel to us through the woods. Looking back once, I was pretty sure I spotted a dark, tall figure in the trees probably 100 feet or more behind us."

"I said to Glenn, 'I think I see it. The thing is *huge*. We better get out of here right away.'"

Linda reported that the couple picked up their pace at this point and broke into a full-out run toward the car. That's when they heard the deep snarl again—and this time it was thunderously loud. At that moment, they were certain that the creature had followed them and may have been within approximately 50 feet of them, while still staying mostly behind the trees.

"As we were almost to the end of the trail connecting with the parking area," resumed Linda, "we heard a sharp huff or angry bark behind us and we both turned around and stopped momentarily. What we saw wasn't too welcoming."

There, partially obscured behind a very large tree, as Linda described, stood a huge creature, at least eight feet in height by Linda and Glenn's estimates, even though it appeared to be slightly bent over. The creature had one big hand and arm partially around the tree that the couple could clearly see, and the animal was looking directly at them. The creature was covered in dark hair, including quite a bit on the face. Its head was very large and somewhat cone-like at the back, reported Glenn.

Soon the bigfoot stepped out from behind the tree, moving directly toward the two picnickers. "Upon seeing this massive, hairy thing come out into the open," resumed Linda, "we turned and broke into a full run again, quickly getting to the car. Still running, Glenn unlocked the doors via his remote fob and we jumped into the car right away. Glenn started the car and punched the gas so we could get out of there as soon as possible. We sped out of this park like bats out of hell—though I'm not too sure how fast bats go. I'll bet we went faster, anyway."

And that was that.

Upon the conclusion of Glenn and Linda's tale, Charlie waited and took a few bites of French toast, smiling with appreciation at each of the witnesses as he chewed. After his big breakfast bite, he took a deep breath and exhaled vociferously.

"Well my, my, that's certainly a novel experience you had there," he said in an empathetic yet fervent fashion.

"I guess you could say that," replied Glenn. "I thought we might die out there, frankly," he continued, somberly.

"My goodness. But speaking of 'out there,'" said Charlie, "Would you mind showing me the location where you had your sighting?"

All was silent at the breakfast table for several extended moments. At other tables, silverware continued to clink off plates and bowls. Much coffee was poured. The buzz of conversations reverberated off the high ceilings.

"I guess we could do that," replied Linda eventually, with less than a smidgeon of enthusiasm.

Charlie could clearly sense the hesitation.

"Oh, I'm sure everything will be fine," he assured. "Whatever was there that day surely isn't there now. These creatures move around quite a bit, you know."

The couple seemed relatively unmoved.

"Um, I really don't know *what* they do," said Linda finally, in a quiet voice.

"Well, I'd be glad to drive us all over to the spot where you had your sasquatch sighting. Just show me the way," said Charlie with encouragement.

"Yeah, I guess that'd be fine," replied Glenn, again with a miniscule modicum of interest.

The three breakfast chums split their bill and walked out of the restaurant to the expansive parking lot and a clear, sunny, breezy day. Charlie lugged his backpack and his beagle bag with bacon.

He led the way over to where Motor Myrtle was parked. Upon getting there and opening up, Charlie of course introduced his investigative partner, who rapidly ran down the RV steps and onto the pavement.

"This is my boss, Betty," Charlie said lovingly of his canine companion.

"Well hi there, Betty," said Linda enthusiastically as she reached down to pet Betty, then climbed up into the RV, followed by Glenn. They took second-row bench seats on opposing sides of the rig. Betty followed Linda to her seat, jumped up into her lap and enjoyed some hands-on affection.

Starting the engine and beginning to cross the parking lot, Charlie said dramatically, "Betty will see to your security and satisfaction as we investigate the goings on here."

Charlie drove around a few bends in the access road and soon asked Glenn where to head. Glenn directed Charlie around a few additional turns, then said, "Right here's the place." It wasn't far at all.

Motor Myrtle pulled into a small gravel parking lot and stopped at the head of a trail.

Meanwhile, Linda had been greatly enjoying some off-trail snuggle time with Betty. Those big, floppy beagle ears were an irresistible scratching target. Even Glenn reached across the aisle and engaged in some comforting canine cuddles.

Exiting the RV, the foursome (with Betty on leash) walked down the trail and, before long, over to the covered picnic table where Linda and Glenn previously had their dinner interrupted by a fusillade of stones.

"This is the place," said Linda, as she looked somewhat warily around the clearing which was ringed by large trees. "I didn't think we'd ever be back here, but whatever."

Meanwhile, Charlie scanned the ground around the A-frame-covered picnic table. He quickly noticed that a number of small rocks, along with one rock about the size of a duckpin bowling ball, were scattered in the grass surrounding the picnic area. He leaned down and picked up the large rock.

"I assume this was the quite sizeable projectile that came your way," ventured Charlie to Glenn and Linda as he held up the prize-worthy monster missile. "I've heard that massive rock throwers can prove hazardous to one's health."

Glenn shook his head affirmatively and said, "Yeah, that's the rock all right. A few feet in a different direction and it could have been the end of one or both of us."

"I'm certainly glad that you were unhurt," added Charlie with a sincerely empathetic tone. He took some photos of the site.

"So," he continued, "Let's head back up the trail, and please let me know when we've reached the spot where you were standing when you saw the bigfoot."

The group then walked to the tree line and just into the woods a bit on the trail. It didn't take long. It wasn't even 30 seconds until they reached the spot.

"It was right here," offered Linda. "We were carrying all our dinner gear and running when we heard the growl or bark or whatever it was back there."

"And it was right behind that big tree there, mostly," said Glenn as he pointed to a tall, thick oak.

Charlie stood still, scratched his beard and asked, "Would you mind taking a stick and showing me on the tree how high you'd estimate the creature's head was?"

For the second time that day, utter silence ensued.

"Uh, okay, okay," said Glenn with the perkiness of someone about to be thrown into a vat of angry poisonous snakes.

He walked over toward the tree, picking up a four- to five-foot-long broken branch along the way.

When Glenn got to the tree, about 60 feet away (while looking nervously around the area), Linda said, "Glenn, you look like a toddler compared to how tall that creature was."

"A toddler, you say?" asked Charlie without particularly expecting a reply.

"That thing was just huge," said Linda.

Betty barked excitedly at a squirrel passing through the area, likely seeking a snack. As with many of the inter-species encounters here, one animal found it expedient to flee toward safer ground.

Looking back at Glenn, Charlie and Linda saw him extend his arm and the branch slowly upward to estimate the height of the creature.

When Glenn stopped the upward motion of the branch and held it still, Charlie shouted to him, "That looks like nearly nine feet to me." This was, of course a non-scientific measurement effort.

Still standing like an awkward and deeply uncomfortable Statue of Liberty, Glenn said, "Yeah, no big surprise. It was truly a monster." Charlie snapped a photo of the extended Glenn.

With that, Glenn pitched the branch off to the side and quickly strode back to the others in the group. He seemed to prefer proximity with people over the lonely memory of a huge monster just down the trail.

Charlie looked about somewhat to see if any footprints were visible on the trail, but he couldn't see any in the thick green brush, weeds and leaf litter covering the trail.

The group began walking up the trail together toward the parking lot. Betty pulled somewhat backward on her leash, still interested in the wayward squirrel.

"Come on, girl, keep it moving," urged Charlie.

As the group neared Motor Myrtle, Charlie said to Linda and Glenn, "Well, thank you so much for sharing your account with me. This was very enlightening, and I must say that I'm glad you came out of it okay."

"So are we," said Linda in conclusion. "I know neither of us ever wants to see something like that again."

With that, the group arrived at the RV. Charlie made the short drive back to the lodge/conference center, and dropped the couple at their car.

"Best of luck to you out there, Charlie," said Linda kindly. Glenn didn't offer additional commentary, as Charlie would have expected.

Charlie then piloted Motor Myrtle the short distance to the RV and camping area.

In the very early evening, Charlie once again raided the RV's freezer and came up with a hotdog dinner to cook over an outdoor campfire. He found some cobs of corn wrapped in aluminum foil that he added to the barbecue. It was a relaxing, smoky, quiet evening in the wooded campground.

After dinner, Charlie and Betty took a walk around the grounds amidst the sunset. As it was now October, Charlie could feel the first hints of impending winter in the air.

After night fell and Betty and Charlie were getting comfortable in bed, Charlie opened the RV window that was right above him and listened very carefully to the sounds of the night. Linda and Glenn's encounter had been quite close to this spot, and Charlie couldn't help but envision hairy, unsupervised creatures approximately nine feet tall roaming the woods here.

Drifting off to sleep, Charlie remembered some SSDD reports saying that bigfoots had been spotted at Salt Fork as close as the edge of the main parking lot. This prospect made for some colorful dreaming content.

The next morning, over a fairly luxurious breakfast back at the lodge restaurant, Charlie worked on his laptop and reviewed the next likely destination on the duo's monstrous magical mystery tour. A brief SSDD report said that a horseback rider in rural Illinois had a close run-in with a sasquatch, and Motor Myrtle would soon begin the trek west.

9

PAWNEE PONY PERIL

The straight westerly route to central Illinois—specifically to Sangamon County just south of Springfield—would take Charlie and Betty over seven hours to make. They took I-70 west to about halfway through Indiana and went right through the big city of Indianapolis, where the travel group stopped for lunch at a fairly trendy microbrew pub. Charlie had some splendid fried chicken, homemade biscuits and a tall blonde pilsner beer. Afterward, Betty got some brewery biscuit bits; no beer for the beagle.

Following the leisurely high-caloric meal, the group resumed their westward travel out of Indy, finally heading south at Springfield, Illinois on I-55 toward the village of Pawnee. They neared their destination late on this October day.

Just off IL-104, Motor Myrtle pulled into Sangchris Lake State Park and its Hickory Point Campground. It was a very pleasant wooded preserve, where after pulling in, Charlie got Motor Myrtle to the reserved pad and completed his requisite RV hookups. As usual the plan was to take Betty out for an extended walk.

However, as soon as they stepped out of the RV, Betty spotted a flock of resident geese in the grass, well across the compound. She charged to the end of her leash and unloaded some boisterous beagle bays at the big black-necked birds. She clearly wanted to chase off the gaggle of geese, but Charlie kept her on-leash and fairly frustrated as she champed at the bit and growled.

"Take it easy, girl," said Charlie to Betty. "There's no need for all this racket. Those big birds haven't done anything offensive to you—at least not yet—so please let them be."

Charlie's admonitions were dutifully ignored by the dog. Charlie tried walking her in the opposite direction to minimize the beagle-toward-bird bellowing, but Betty seemed intent on moving more like a brick than a beagle.

After many hours of travel and tugging, both dog and driver were soon quite tired, so they settled down and turned in not too long after their frozen dinner of meatloaf, corn and mashed potatoes. Betty, of course, got a pinch of leftover meatloaf in addition to her usual dinnertime kibble.

Before bed, Charlie texted the subsequent witness, a young lady who he'd be meeting in Pawnee Village the next day for lunch. In a text reply, she recommended a pizza place in town as a meeting spot. Charlie, of course, acceded to this suggestion without hesitation.

Early the next morning after a breakfast consisting of frozen boxed pancakes and some bacon, Charlie and Betty took a lengthy walk at Sangchris Lake. The area was beautiful for a stroll, featuring countless sizeable trees on the bank of the huge, picturesque body of water. Betty remained deeply interested in goosing the geese population in one area of the compound, but Charlie held on tight, redirected, and kept her from excessively badgering the big birds.

Targeting the appointed hour of the late morning, Charlie and Betty drove into the village of Pawnee to meet the witness at a restaurant called Casey's Pizza. After pulling into the parking lot of the small one-story building, Charlie closed up the rig and got Betty settled for a bit of a wait.

Charlie entered Casey's establishment carrying his backpack and wearing his wide-brimmed fedora with bigfooter's badge, and since he was such a distinctly unfamiliar sight in these local environs, a twenty-something female apparently figured out who he was right away.

A not-tall young lady with cute, short blonde hair walked up toward Charlie with her hands in her back pockets. Charlie observed that the girl was wearing dusty blue jeans, a flannel shirt and cowboy boots—perhaps an outdoor woman of the Midwest. She quickly spoke to Charlie.

"Are you Mr. Marlowe?" she asked cheerfully.

"Why yes, young lady, you must be Sharon Greenwald."

"That's right. It's good to meet you," said Sharon, offering a warm smile.

Charlie swelled with genteel pleasantness. "And it's fully splendid to meet you as well, Ms. Greenwald," he said gushingly as he shook her hand and bowed down graciously.

"Oh, just call me Sharon," she replied with a slight giggle at Charlie's overly courtly behavior. "Would you care to join me at my table?"

"I'd be delighted," answered Charlie as he followed Sharon to one of the booths lining each side of the eatery. Eight or ten freestanding tables inhabited the center portion of the room. Plentiful sunlight streamed in from the big windows on one side of the establishment, and the discussion duo would be taking a window-side seat. Just a few other diners were scattered about the room at this pre-lunchtime hour.

"This place has some of the best pizza you'll find anywhere around here," explained Sharon as they took their seats. "I've been coming here since I was a teenager, and the place never gets old to me."

"I'm quite glad to hear that," said Charlie. "Truly good pizza can seem like a gift from the gods, and good God I'm hungry," he said vigorously, laughing at his own gluttonous inclinations.

A late teenage male server carrying an order pad came up to the booth and asked if Charlie and Sharon were ready for beverages. Sharon ordered a diet cola, and Charlie decided that such a cutback on sugar might be a good idea; he ordered the same thing.

"I'll need to unfurl my portable technology, if you don't mind," said Charlie as he pulled his laptop from the backpack, opened it and powered up.

"Sure, that's fine, Charlie," replied Sharon.

As Charlie continued to get settled, he said, "So, from what I understand, your encounter involved an equine element."

Sharon looked at him blankly for a moment. Then, as comprehension germinated, she replied, "Oh yes, I was on my horse Trooper when we saw that creature in the woods."

"That must have been quite a shock," editorialized Charlie, still getting himself settled for notetaking.

Sharon nodded her head in the affirmative and pursed her bright red lips for several seconds. Eventually she replied, "You have no idea."

The server returned with the beverages and asked if Sharon and Charlie were ready to order their lunch. They each ordered a small personal pan-sized pizza, with Charlie ordering pepperoni and mushrooms on his, and Sharon ordering sausage, mushrooms and onions on hers. As more and more patrons were launching their lunch orders, the environment was starting to smell quite enticing.

After finishing the order with the server, Charlie sat back for a moment until Sharon appeared ready to share her tale. His fingers hovered over the computer keyboard in anticipation of the retelling.

Sharon launched into her account, with Charlie taking copious notes.

Setting the scene, Sharon said the day had been mostly sunny, just before dusk, when she was riding her Morgan quarter horse mix, Trooper, along a heavily wooded though well-established trail not far from Pawnee. He was a big, healthy, majestic horse—chestnut-brown in color. They had been out trotting slowly and peacefully for about a half an hour amidst the large, lush, leafy trees, when suddenly, Trooper stopped dead in his tracks on the dirt trail they were on and stared straight ahead into the woods.

Upon the surprisingly quick stop, Sharon lunged forward somewhat and looked in the same direction as the horse did, and to her surprise, she saw a tall, dark-colored animal powerfully striding straight towards them through the woods. The creature was so large that upon quick observation, Sharon estimated that the creature's head was roughly at the same height as hers—even though she was sitting atop a large horse. She didn't know what type of colossal being this was but she was very concerned that whatever it was, it seemed to have malicious or at least aggressive intent as it approached.

Once the creature got within about 30 yards of horse and rider, Trooper reared back in fearful response. (This physical reaction was well outside of the horse's typical behavior.) Sharon reported that she had to grab wildly for the saddle horn and tighten her grip on the horse's reins in order to not be pitched backward off the horse. As Sharon described, once the horse's front hooves landed on the ground again, Trooper instantly turned and began sprinting in the opposite direction. He clearly had no taste for mixing it up with a mysterious, gigantic forest monster of undetermined origin.

Sharon said that Trooper pounded down the trail at full speed. She held on for dear life. The unexpected turnabout and flight were shocking to her. She soon looked to her right, and to her utter surprise and horror, the now-running creature had quickly caught up to the galloping horse.

"I got a real good look at him then," said Sharon to Charlie. "It was definitely a bigfoot or sasquatch…whatever the right word is for those things. Never in my life did I think I'd see something like that."

Now with a better view of the creature's body, Sharon realized she was observing something far beyond the typical.

"Soon he closed in and was just about ten feet to my right as Trooper charged all crazy down the trail," Sharon continued. "The creature easily kept up with us, and I can't tell you how scared that made me. It was so physically far outside of anything I'd experienced before. He had huge, long arms and legs. His torso was like…the size of a refrigerator or something. He was looking right over at me and sort of snorting out of this big wide nose. God, it was incredible," she said, shaking her head.

Sharon hesitated for several extended seconds, likely re-experiencing her forest flight.

"Another weird sensation," continued Sharon rapidly, "was that with every step this thing took, there was a sort of thunderous boom that seemed to shoot out across the woods. Even though Trooper is big and makes plenty of hoof noise when he runs, I could still hear and feel these massive thuds with every step the bigfoot took…like maybe this creature weighed as much as my horse!"

Sharon didn't know if she and her horse were about to be victims of a monster attack. She hoped not, but the creature was *very* fast and *very* close, she told Charlie. The further they ran, the closer toward the horse the creature veered. Ultimately the creature wasn't more than five feet from the horse and rider.

Since the cover of woods continued almost to the area of Sharon's residence and barn, the fearful chase continued for several minutes.

"Trooper looked over every few seconds and, I'm sure, saw this creature," added Sharon. "He lowered his head and seemed to want to put things in a higher gear to get away, but I knew the poor guy was already at full speed. I know he was confused and scared. I sure was."

Sharon offered additional description of the creature. "You know, as this thing was running next to us and getting closer, I had no idea what it intended to do. Its arms and legs were so gigantically muscular that it could have killed me and my horse in seconds, I'm sure. At the time I wasn't sure why it didn't. It seemed kind of angry or possessive or something. The creature had long dark hair that just flowed back behind it as it ran. I could see the face very clearly. It looked ape-like, and also sort of human-like, as it focused on us. Regardless, the face and head were really big. *Everything* on it was big."

"That must have been a truly awful fright for you," Charlie said to Sharon simply.

"You better believe it was. We finally came out of the woods and into my neighborhood. Once we got out in the open sunlight, the bigfoot peeled off to its right and stopped chasing us, for goodness sake. We got up onto the street, still at full speed, and followed that for a few hundred yards until we were back home. The mailboxes flew past pretty quickly. I was *so* glad that we hadn't been further out on a miles-long ride that day."

At this point in Sharon's monologue, the pizza server returned with the two hot micro-pies. Charlie was quite enthralled by Sharon's descriptions, but he was also up for some pepperoni pleasure.

"Here you go, folks," said the young server as he walked up, scooping up the pies from his tray and placing them on the table—first for Sharon and then for Charlie.

"Oh, that looks absolutely delightful, son!" said Charlie. He was quite ready to plow his personal pizza.

The young man looked at Charlie with an uncertain gaze, then made his way back to the kitchen.

Getting set and taking some initial bites, Sharon continued her account. "Anyway, we got to our property and fence, and I looked around to see if the monster was still anywhere around. He wasn't. I suppose he headed back into the woods. I jumped down, opened the gate and shooed Trooper right into the paddock and barn. He seemed really happy to get into that barn. I don't blame him a bit. He hit up his water tank right away and didn't come outside the rest of the day, poor fellow."

Sharon had one more detail of her perilous pony pursuit to recount. "I got inside the house, took off my hair clip and boots, and headed straight to the bar. I poured the biggest shot of whiskey that I could handle, and downed a few of them, actually, before I started to settle down a little bit. And I'm no fan of whiskey," she reported in humorous summary.

"Hmm," said Charlie, contemplating the terminus of the trail terror, and not so much the self-administered spirit sedative. "Well, Sharon, would you say there was any evidence left of the creature's presence...footprints, hair on a fence, a broken gate...anything like that?"

After a few pensive seconds, Sharon said, "No, I can't say that the monster left much of anything behind."

Having heard and documented the very detailed recounting of the strange event and the apparent lack of extant evidence, Charlie wasn't exactly sure of what to do since the account seemed to come to a close. Then, to Charlie's surprise, Sharon made the decision for him.

She said, "Um, Mr. Marlowe, what I've just told you isn't exactly the end of the story, you know." Sharon delivered this statement in a deadly serious tone, offering just the tiniest hint of a secretive grin.

"Oh no?" asked Charlie, looking up from his personal pie with curiosity.

"Oh no," replied Sharon resolutely. "We had other...interactions with this creature...soon enough."

Charlie was stunned at this revelation, so much so that he actually stopped eating momentarily.

"Well, please enlighten me!"

"So, later I walked back out to the barn to check on Trooper," Sharon said. "This was quite an unusual trauma he'd been through and I wanted to make sure he was okay."

"When I got out to him, I refilled his feed bin and water, and gave him all kinds of rubdown attention... like I did some grooming on him with a brush. I rubbed his face and chin so we could have some quiet, safe time together. I pulled up each of his hooves to make sure he hadn't gotten hurt or anything during that crazy fast chase we went through. Fortunately he seemed fine. I also spent some time with his roan donkey roommate, Zeke. He was pretty as a picture standing at rest in his stall."

"Zeke," remarked Charlie. "What an excellent name for a burro boy."

"Yep," said Sharon, continuing. "He's quite the clown. But anyway, right before bedtime I went out to check on Trooper one more time. It was a cool, clear night, probably about 9:30 or so. I brought Trooper and Zeke each a carrot, and rubbed them down a little more. Trooper seemed pretty pleased to see me at that point, and he was much more settled down than earlier. I imagine he was happy to be safely back in his stall and ready for bed just like me. I've often found that Zeke can calm him down pretty effectively," she added with a slight laugh. "Silly donkey pals can be a real help."

"Oh, I believe that," agreed Charlie. "I'd have one at home if I had room, but my wife Francesca says we already have one too many asses on the premises." Sharon giggled at that statement.

Sharon reported that she gave the big horse one final pat and then shut down the lights and locked the barn door, returning to the house.

"So that was it for that wacky day," said Sharon to Charlie.

Charlie waited a bit, then asked as gently as possible, "I'm not quite sure what else remarkable happened that you were referring to, Sharon."

She giggled a bit more.

"Well okay, Charlie; I wasn't done. Real early the next morning I headed out to do all my barn chores and the like, but as I walked up to the barn, I immediately noticed that the big padlock had been broken off. It was lying in pieces in the dirt right in front of the swinging doors. Weird."

"Oh my, that's a concern," said Charlie with prompt empathy.

"Yeah, tell me about it. Stuff like that *never* happens around here, and of course I feared the worst when it came to my hooved buddies. I swung that door open wide and ran inside the barn like it was the end of the world."

"I can understand your great panic," said Charlie.

"But as I took a few steps inside—into the dusty dark of the morning sun in the barn—I could see that Trooper was standing there pretty much asleep and was just fine. I patted him on the butt to wake him up a little. Then I jogged over to Zeke's pen and he also was fine. I was *so* relieved."

Charlie's fingers hovered over the keyboard again as he awaited the import of this part of Sharon's account. He had no idea where the tale was going.

"So I went back to Trooper and started to run my hands down his back" she said. "Right away I noticed, in his mane, several new braids in his hair."

"Braids?!" exclaimed Charlie reflexively and swiftly.

"That's right. He had these beautiful hair braids hanging parallel to each other in his mane. I couldn't believe it."

"Braids in his mane, you say?!" said Charlie, not quite grasping the import of what Sharon was describing now.

"Yes. On each side of his mane, starting from the top, he had three fairly large braids hanging down. On each braid, the hair had been twisted around probably five or six times. Then at the bottom of each one, below the last of the interwoven braids, the hair straightened out again and ended."

"Good gracious," replied Charlie. "And who do you believe would have done such a thing overnight?"

"Well, of course I can't be sure," said Sharon, "but I don't think a person did this horse braid work. To begin with, the lock outside had been obliterated, and I didn't see any scratches on it or marks of a cutting tool being used. Honestly it looked like the lock had just been ripped apart by hand or something...like you would a piece of stale old bread."

Charlie just stared at Sharon.

"And here's more," she said. "This clearly happened in the middle of the night. I had been out there late the night before, then quite early the next morning. The horse and donkey were utterly unharmed. The braids on Trooper were quite obvious but not all that sophisticated, really. I know because I used to have longer hair and could do things with it." (She laughed somewhat.) "Why would someone in this little neighborhood break into our barn and put exactly six braids into my horse's mane...only hours after we had been chased almost all the way back here by a big, nosy monster?"

The light began to go on for Charlie at this point. "Ah, you think the *bigfoot* returned and did this," he exclaimed.

"I do, Charlie," she said, laughing a bit more at the astonishing development she was describing.

"You know, your thinking on this sounds pretty sound to me," said Charlie approvingly if not redundantly. "But I must ask: Do you have any photos or other evidence of these braids?" He delivered this query with a great deal of hope.

"Well, I never did take any pictures of the braids," Sharon said, "but this didn't happen all that long ago, and I never undid them or anything. They're still on the long brown hair of my big, glamorous Mr. Trooper."

Charlie stared at Sharon with wide eyes. Her next statement didn't disappoint.

"If you want, we can go back to the barn and I'll show you," she said.

Charlie nearly flipped his laptop, fumbled his fedora and spilled his soda in response to Sharon's offer.

"That would be *stupendous*!" he said with delight.

Sharon and Charlie each took their final bites of pizza and finished up with swigs of soda. Since there were some pizza crust shards left over, Charlie scooped them up as he was summoning the server, who provided a small to-go box. Charlie closed up and stowed his laptop, paid the restaurant bill and walked outside with Sharon.

"Please give me a moment while I share some pizza pieces with my copilot," Charlie said to Sharon. "Then I can follow you back to your residence."

As Charlie was climbing up into the RV, Sharon inquired, "Your *copilot*? Who's that?"

Charlie didn't hear her or respond.

So, Sharon walked over to her car. Meanwhile Charlie unlocked the RV and handed several pieces of pizza crust to a clearly appreciative Betty, who had been sleeping on one of the comfy single beds. The dog had to chew with hefty, exaggerated mouth chomps to wrestle the puffy breaded crusts down into her belly. The effort, however, was entirely worth it to her.

Charlie then got Motor Myrtle started and he backed out of his parking space. Sharon did the same in her small car, and she led the way on the drive back to her home and barn.

Arriving at Sharon's rural development, which was ringed by large trees in the distance but not as many near the spread-out ranch-type homes, Charlie pulled Motor Myrtle into a dirt and gravel driveway behind Sharon's car. As the travelers pulled in, a two-story house sat to the left, and a small tan barn to the right. Charlie liked the looks of this rural donkey-and-horse haven. The afternoon was sunny and cool, the fragrance of hay and manure ubiquitous, and the suburban-country setting appealing to Charlie's well-traveled eyes.

Sharon had gotten quickly out of her car, and Charlie soon descended the RV steps with Betty on leash.

"This is my aforementioned overseer and directional ace, Betty," said Charlie with his customary flair for words.

"Oh, hi Betty!" said Sharon eagerly. She bent down and gave the little tricolor hound some affectionate nuzzling about the head and ears. Betty immediately took to Sharon, as she often did to anyone who seemed animal oriented. "She is *so* cute."

"Yes, but like me," he replied, "she's been eating rather luxuriously on this trip and may not fit into her tiara by the time we return home."

Sharon, still rubbing down the plump, happy beagle, laughed gleefully at Charlie's imaginative commentary.

"Do you mind if I take her for a brief walk before we head in?" asked Charlie.

"Oh, of course not. Take as much time as you'd like."

With that, Charlie led Betty back out the driveway next to a fence line. Nose to the ground, the dog seemed to pick up countless scents as she proceeded (as hunting dogs always do), and her sniffer clearly went into overdrive discerning the smells of probable donkeys, horses, other dogs, cats, birds and unidentified creatures that had passed through the area recently.

After a few minutes, Charlie took Betty back to the RV and got her suitably situated. He decided to leave her there instead of potentially causing any upset in the equine quarters.

Charlie then jogged back toward the barn, where Sharon was waiting. She put a key into the obviously new padlock—the replacement for the one torn off the hasp by...someone or something. Charlie didn't miss this detail.

Sharon energetically swung the barn doors wide open, and she and Charlie walked inside. The air there was dark and dusty, with a flood of muck and mammal odors.

Trooper was the closest animal of interest as Charlie and Sharon proceeded inward toward the left side of the barn. The big horse turned around as they approached, looking somewhat intently at Charlie, the newest interloper.

"Hi big boy, how are you doing today?" asked Sharon as she put hands upon the haunches of the sizeable quadruped.

"Oh, he's a beautiful boy, you know," said Charlie in obvious appreciation of the big brown horse.

"Yes, and check out this hairdo," added Sharon as she tugged gently upon a braid on one side of the horse's mane.

Charlie leaned in and inspected the hairstyle artistry. As he stepped closer, he realized just how large Trooper was compared to the puniness of humans.

"That's *quite* impressive," he said as he grasped one of the braids hanging off the huge creature next to him.

"And if you think about who could have taken the time—in the middle of the night—to stand here and gently do this handiwork, it's pretty incredible," said Sharon. "I don't feel so great about someone breaking into the barn, but at least no other harm was done."

Charlie thought about this some more, and in the presence of the large equine, fully realized what he was witnessing.

"It's completely incredible that the bigfoot creature found its way to the barn, broke in here and did this," said Charlie as he ran the horse's braids through his fingers. "He really must have become instantly interested in this horse when in the woods and decided to follow you guys home, albeit at a distance, ultimately. Then at night, he must have made some fast, deep peace with Trooper in order to weave this magic here."

"Magic it is," agreed Sharon. "He must have done something pretty profound to calm Trooper down after the earlier pursuit. I don't understand it at all. I sure wish Trooper could talk...and tell me all about how this weird, huge monster came in here and saw to the horse's hairstyle."

Charlie could only shake his head at the thought of what must have happened between the large creatures.

Switching gears, Sharon said, "Come and meet Zeke, too. Oh, and over in the corner there are the busted lock pieces," she said helpfully as she pointed to a very dark corner of the barn. Charlie walked over and looked down, trying to inspect the dark metal detritus in the corner of the barn. There wasn't much to see.

After a few moments, the pair walked around to the next stall, where Charlie made the acquaintance of the grayish donkey.

"Well, it's great to meet you, Zeke," said Charlie kindly to the good-sized, sturdily built donkey. Upon receiving some head pats, back scratches and chin rubs from Charlie, the donkey let loose an enormous ten-second bray ("*Hon*-kee *hon*-kee!") at full volume that very nearly shook the walls of the barn before its descrescendo into a low, guttural blast.

"Wow, he's got quite the singing voice," said Charlie to Sharon, who had no reason to differ.

After spending some more cuddling and laughing time with the lively donkey, Charlie walked back to Trooper and took out his camera to document the horse's braid work. He took several photos from different angles on each side of the horse's neck. The hairy braids were attractive and mysterious at the same time.

"Thank you so much for allowing me to observe this incredible artistry," said Charlie to Sharon as he finished up with his photos. Charlie had heard about bigfoot braid work before but had never witnessed any of it himself. This would prove to be yet another valuable piece of distinctive evidence from this multi-state, multi-creature expedition.

Charlie took one close look down at the dirt in the barn and could see that the many horse and donkey hoof prints had long since obliterated any sasquatch footprints that may have existed previously. However, the horse braid photos were something new altogether, and, clearly a gem of evidence.

Back outside, Charlie expressed his thanks and said his goodbyes to Sharon.

"This has been an *amazing* experience," he said to the lively young woman.

"Getting chased and then braided by a bigfoot isn't something I would have expected in my horsey life," said Sharon, with ample smiles, to the kindly older man at her side.

"I'm very appreciative that you shared this with me, Sharon. Plus, the pizza at Casey's was superb. Betty just loved the gourmet crusts!"

Sharon laughed yet again at the eccentric, friendly man.

At this point, Sharon gave Charlie a gentle hug and parted with him in order to close up her barn. Charlie headed back to the oft-hungry traveling companion/canine awaiting him in the RV.

Climbing back into the big rig, Charlie fired up Motor Myrtle and headed slowly out of the rural neighborhood, taking in the views of each lovely ranch property along the way.

Charlie and Betty then traveled a few miles back to the Hickory Point Campground for some outdoor lakeside time, goose gandering, and late-night relaxation with a cool breeze coming in off the water.

For the first time in about a day, Charlie reviewed whatever communication may have arrived via phone, text or email. That day, Jimmy at the SSDD had sent him an email with a link to a very fresh SSDD report from central Wisconsin, where some fellow RV travelers had had a late-night encounter with an apparent sasquatch. They had agreed to wait in place if an investigator was available to meet with them soon. Sitting in the RV and pondering the travel task at hand, Charlie replied and said he'd be up for a rapid departure from Pawnee.

First, however, a bit more relaxation was indicated. After closing down the electronics, Charlie grabbed a can of sparkling lime water from the fridge and sipped it in a lounge chair as the sun dropped over the horizon. Betty continued to prowl for geese until dark.

10

CLOSE CALL AT THE CAMPER

Early the next day, Motor Myrtle headed north out of Pawnee, taking highways I-55 to I-39 north. The travelers stayed on I-39 for an extended period as they paralleled the huge Lake Michigan.

With his stomach starting to growl a bit, Charlie piloted Motor Myrtle to a stop in the town of Rockford. There at a cozy café he grabbed a succulent crab cake lunch along with a cold IPA beer called Foggy Geezer. (He thought that was a fittingly eponymous name for his main beverage of the day.) He tipped the big, hazy beer back with gusto as he noshed on seafood. Afterward, stepping out of the restaurant to return to the parked RV, Charlie burped like a hippo and brought Betty some terrifically tasty tidbits of crab cake.

Exiting Rockford, Motor Myrtle accessed I-90 north, then eventually took US-151 to Waupun, Wisconsin, in Dodge County—about 70 miles northwest of Milwaukee. The traveling crew put in over 300 miles and five hours of highway driving that day.

Charlie had researched the local area somewhat, learning that Myrtle's destination was adjacent to the Horicon Marsh Wildlife Refuge— renowned as the largest cattail marsh in the United States. In fact there were many lakes and wildlife reserves throughout this region. Thus, Charlie knew that the scenery here, despite the non-sunbathing temperatures, would be appealing.

Charlie also had learned that witness contacts in Wisconsin had their creature sighting in a nearby rural RV park known as the Playful Goose, so Charlie and Betty headed directly goose-ward to begin their investigation. (Charlie noted that big birds seemed to appear frequently on this trip. Betty didn't restrain her woof-based commentary.)

Just before pulling into the park, Charlie stopped and rang the phone number he had been provided for Jorge and Mary Gutierrez. Charlie talked via cellphone with Mary, who told him where the couple's RV was parked. She provided a description. The Gutierrez rig differed from Charlie's RV in that it was apparently a fifth wheeler, i.e., a detached trailer pulled by a pickup truck. Motor Myrtle, in contrast, was a one-piece wonder.

The rig pulled into the park, and Charlie was immediately taken by the wooded setting and its proximity to the Rock River. It was an Autumn day, just starting to cool off a bit, and Charlie could clearly visualize how pretty the area would be in the warmer months. He checked in at the office and headed toward his parking spot. Fortunately there were few campers in the park at this juncture, so Charlie was able to secure a pad quite close to the Gutierrez' RV. He spotted, not too far away, the rig that Mary had described on the phone.

Myrtle settled in at the appointed camping spot, and Charlie attended to hook-up chores after taking Betty for a leisurely walk about the grounds. Although the season was late, Charlie figured he and his dog might spot a few Canada geese here. There apparently were hundreds of thousands of such birds in the area in the spring and fall. They did indeed spot a few stragglers, and Betty got in some hefty barks.

Quite late in the day, Charlie walked Betty over to the witness couple's stylish white and black Durango RV, with a large green Ford pickup adjacent. (The front of the RV was upheld by stabilizer legs used when the rig is detached.) Charlie brought along his usual retinue of backpack and beagle.

Charlie rapped on the door, which was toward the rear of the vehicle, and a good-looking, fairly young Hispanic man with a dark, trim beard answered the knock. He introduced himself as Jorge, and soon after, his wife Mary came to the door to meet Charlie.

"It's nice to meet you both," said Charlie. "This is my hench-person, Betty."

With that, Jorge quickly disappeared into the vehicle for a moment, and returned with his own copilot.

"And this is Gizzard!" he said brightly.

Bounding wildly out of the RV door and down onto the ground came Gizzard, a small, off-white Shih Tzu dog with a crazily hairy face. He and Betty instantly took to each other—nuzzling, sniffing and cartwheeling about.

The assembled group of humans got plenty of laughs as the crazed canines cavorted.

Clad in blue jeans and a multi-colored floral pattern shirt, Mary said, "Mr. Giz thinks he owns the whole place, so I'm sure it will be good for him to have a buddy here."

"Come on in, Charlie," said Jorge, who was wearing dark jeans, a black Harley Davidson t-shirt and brown cowboy-ish boots. "But first I need to catch the little whirlwind here." He briefly pursued Gizzard around the vehicle before finally scooping him up into his arms and carrying the dog back into the RV.

Charlie unclipped Betty and let her twirl around the inside of the vehicle with Gizzard at will. Charlie and the Gutierrez couple sat down at the RV's dining table.

Betty and Gizzard provided ample background noise consisting of playful squeaks, yips and miniature growls.

"So, tell me about your stay here, if you don't mind," said Charlie to Mary and Jorge. As he said this, he extracted his laptop from his bag and got it set up. After a minute or so, he was ready to proceed.

"Well, we're from down near Chicago, and we wanted to come up and experience some country we hadn't seen before," said Jorge, who spoke with a level, fairly soft voice. His wife also was not a terribly loud person.

"This is a great spot," said Mary, "but we ran into something we didn't expect to see. Our planned stay was for five days and nights, but it didn't take very long before we had a very strange meeting on a cold night."

"Well, regardless," said Charlie, "I'm very glad you chose to remain here after reporting your encounter. Most often, witnesses out on the road aren't able to stay in place after they've had their sighting and informed the SSDD."

"What's the SSDD?" asked Mary.

"Oh, I apologize," said Charlie with a mild jolt of realization. "That's the Sasquatch Sighting Documentation Database, the website where you reported your bigfoot run-in."

"Ah yes, Jimmy at the organization was pretty helpful as we tried to get our information sent in," said Jorge.

"So anyway, this was our first night at the campground," said Mary, clearly launching into the crux of the couple's monster narrative. "We had been here several hours, barbecued a bit of dinner out on the grill, took Gizzard here for a walk, and turned in for the night. We had been asleep for...I don't know how many hours..."

"It was the middle of the night, anyway," chimed in Jorge.

"Right" she continued, "We were sound asleep when Gizzard started barking like crazy. He was all upset like someone was right outside or something. Both of us got up and started looking out the windows. Jorge walked up to the front of the RV and looked out, and I went to the back and checked the window there. It was almost totally dark except for a little light from near the office across the property."

"As soon as I got to the back door," said Mary, "I was amazed to see that someone big was standing outside, right next to the door—almost plastered to it—trying to look in the window, pretty much. I whispered, probably pretty loudly, to Jorge that there was someone back here and that he should come see. Jorge came right to the back and looked out, and I know he saw the big shadow in the window."

"That's right. It was someone *really* big just standing there looking in," said Jorge. "We both watched this enormous face just standing there right in front of the door, looking at us. Soon I went over to a drawer and grabbed my pistol. I wasn't sure if this person wanted to break in, hurt us, steal something, or whatever."

"So my idea was to get to the back window with my pistol and turn on an outside light—maybe catching this perp in the act," said Jorge. "So I did that, and was just about ready to turn on the light and throw open the back door."

"While Jorge was getting ready," said Mary, "I pulled out my phone and took a photo of the person's face and upper body through the still-closed window. The picture was awfully dark and hard to see, but I thought it was important to try and capture *something* about this person."

"...And you still have this photo, right?" asked Charlie quickly.

"Of course I do. These aren't things that I'll be deleting anytime soon." She handed her phone over to Charlie, who looked very closely at the photo. It revealed a huge, dark, hairy upper body and a rough outline of a head—with two bright eyeballs seemingly boring straight into the RV. The image was very eerie and slightly unsettling. There was no facial detail other than the bright eyes.

"My God, look at that thing," said Charlie in an incredulous tone. He looked down at the image on the phone in his hands, with no immediate inclination to relinquish the phone or its spooky image back to Mary. "And it was just right here outside this very door?!"

"Yeah," said Jorge, "this giant guy was just standing there with penetrating eye shine, like it wanted to come through and eat us or something. But it was completely quiet...there was no sound at all. It was creepy strange. I can't tell you how terrifying this was in the middle of the night."

"And also," added Mary, "there was this strong smell that just covered everything around. It was like...stinky trash and dead fish and skunk leavings...no wonder our Gizzard boy was so upset," she added with a slight giggle.

Charlie soon found that Jorge was nowhere near done describing his impressions.

"And you know," he began again, "as I was standing there looking at this thing, it slowly began to dawn on me that the window we were looking through was *way* too high for anyone to be looking at us through, at my eye level, basically. As my senses returned to me in the middle of the damn night—I guess activated by the crazy stench—I remembered that I had pulled in the retractable step below the back door before closing up for the night—as I always do. So that's when I realized that this high-up face must have been connected to a body that was standing all the way down on the ground—not on the raised retractable step. So, this person or creature must have been absolutely *massive*."

"After a few moments, I reached over and flipped the switch for the outside rear light. It was kind of scary to do, but I wanted to try and step out there and confront this big, stinky thing. I figured once I stepped outside, I'd see the huge man right there, but when I turned on the light and tossed open the door, there wasn't anyone in sight."

Jorge reported hearing bipedal footsteps moving away from the RV at a rather brisk pace, though he couldn't see anyone. He also said that, with the RV's back door now wide open, he heard a few low, heavy grunts as whatever had been there exited the area into the woods. Jorge also heard crunching of leaves and/or twigs as the individual entered the woods.

"Again, this thing sounded just huge, although I didn't know what exactly it was," said Jorge. Apparently he walked a number of steps toward where he heard the footfall sounds diminishing into the woods, but didn't see or hear anything at that point.

Mary resumed the narrative. "Jorge came back in and I asked him if he saw anything. He said 'no' as he quickly closed and locked the back door, then checked all the other doors to boot. At that point he said he was *super* glad to be back in a locked, warm vehicle. I told him there was probably nothing at all to worry about now because we had a very protective dog on board: the fearsome Gizzard." She giggled a bit at her own sarcasm.

"Yeah, and once I settled down a bit," said Jorge, "I said to Gizzard: 'Boy, you would have whooped that big guy's butt, wouldn't you have?'"

Mary said, "We stayed up for a while talking about what had happened. We didn't know whether we should report this to someone, or maybe just leave, or whatever. Regardless, there wasn't a lot we could do in the middle of the night, so we tried to calm down and get some rest."

"That wasn't terribly easy," added Jorge sullenly.

"So, next morning we went outside to look around and see if anything got left or got damaged," said Mary. "We didn't see any damage to the door latch or the truck or anything. It looked like the person or creature must have really wanted to take a look at us but didn't seem to want to break in and cause any harm."

"We did find a few footprints in the dirt between the camper and the truck, though," said Jorge. "They weren't real clear, but you could tell they were made by huge, bare feet…probably like human footprints, but gigantic. I'd say they were more than 13 or 14 inches long. I took a few photos of them, and you can take a look if you'd like."

"That would be great, Jorge," responded Charlie quickly. Jorge handed over his phone and, as usual, Charlie sat very still and looked deeply at the imagery evidence.

"Wow, those are big all right," he said to Jorge. "Can I take copies of these plus the one that Mary took at the window?"

"Sure, that would be fine," replied Mary. Both Gutierrez individuals handed their phones over to Charlie, and he uploaded the photos one by one over to his laptop via a connecting cable.

"Now, can we examine the exterior of the rig and the surrounding area to see if there's anything of interest?"

"Yeah, we can do that," said Jorge, "but there isn't a lot there at this point." Jorge led the other two to the back door and they all stepped outside. Charlie still had his overcoat on. The group left the dog pals inside to fend for themselves for a while. Charlie grabbed his backpack...

After the trio stepped down to ground level outside, Jorge gave Charlie a detailed overview of the retractable step beneath the RV's rear door. Jorge pulled the step out and locked it in place. Charlie looked closely at the step and could see only dusty tennis shoe-type tracks upon the dark metal surface. Nothing organic or unusual was visible on the step. Jorge stepped up onto it and showed Charlie how his own head was perhaps two feet short of the top of the door/window.

Jorge then pushed the step back under the rig and secured it, saying to Charlie, "As I said before, without this step being accessible, the creature that visited us was just standing on the ground here...but his head was almost at the top of the window. God, he must have been huge!"

Charlie took a few steps backward and considered the distance from the ground to the top of the door.

"Well if it was as you said—as I'm sure it was, Jorge—then there's an easy way that we can estimate the creature's height," said Charlie thoughtfully. He reached into his backpack, extracted his tape measure and went to work.

Standing on the ground beneath the back door, Charlie extended the tape measure (in a slightly wobbly fashion) up to the top of the back door. He then extended the remainder of the tape down to the dirt, looking rather like an inebriated condor spreading its wings recklessly. Soon, the tape disconnected from its tenuous clasp at the top lip of the door and fell to the ground.

"Oh, rats," said Charlie with abundant exasperation.

"Here, let me help," said Jorge with alacrity, jogging over to aid Charlie in measuring the vertical distance. He reached as high up as he could, holding the upper segment of the yellow metal tape against the top of the door while Charlie pulled the other end of the tape down toward the dirt again. With a bit more stability in the measurement process this time, Charlie was able to derive a result.

"The top of the window where you saw the face is eight feet, three inches," he said with comfortable certainty.

"Wow, that guy was truly a giant!" said Mary rapidly.

Charlie helped clarify. "Yes, and even if the top of the creature's head wasn't absolutely level with the top of the door, it was surely close, judging from the photo you took. So, an estimate of eight feet in height is readily within the realm of possibility."

"Unbelievable," said Jorge simply, shaking his head as he spoke. "I had no idea that these…creatures…or whatever they are…could be so big. Next time I better make sure Mr. Gizzard is on the case," he added comically.

Riffing off of Jorge's comment, Mary said, "Gizzard could easily take care of something eight feet tall." Jorge and Charlie both stood still in place and looked at her quizzically. "He'd start by lifting his leg on the big thing and soaking him for all he's worth."

Jorge and Charlie got a healthy guffaw out of that comment. Charlie added, "Yes, that would surely chase *me* off."

Regaining his investigative posture, Charlie said, "Let's look around some more, what do you say?"

"Yup, that's fine," replied Jorge, "though there isn't much left, I'm sure."

"Oh, that's okay, I just like to review every corner of an encounter environment," explained Charlie. He began wandering around, looking down at the dirt for visible marks of any kind.

"Let me show you the best print we saw, if it's still here," offered Jorge. He walked about 30 to 40 feet out from the rig toward the woods, scouring the dirt, small rocks and dried leaves along the way.

"Here it is. It's *mostly* still together, though not great," said Jorge as he looked down at a bare dirt spot.

Carrying his backpack, Charlie scurried over to where Jorge was standing and began to review the footprint. It did indeed look like a bare human print, but it was much larger. There were some vague bird or vermin tracks immediately next to the footprint, and plenty of smudges around the perimeter of the track, but at least some evidence of the visiting creature was visible.

"That's *not too bad*," said Charlie. He knelt down next to the track and, as usual, extended his tape measure.

"It's about 15 and a half inches," offered Charlie.

Mary and Jorge looked at each other with amazement.

"Let me get some shots here," said Charlie as he grabbed his camera and angled variously about the print, taking photos from different perspectives as the tape measure remained in place. Kneeling down next to the print, he adopted a didactic tone for the benefit of his witnesses. "You know, if you look closely, you can see several common characteristics of sasquatch-type footprints." Mary and Jorge both stepped in closer for a better view.

"Of course, the overall length is impressive," resumed Charlie, "but look at the shape of the foot. This is what we always see. The heel portion is rounded, but there is no visible arch, as you'd see in a human footprint. It looks all flat. Instead of curving, the rear portion of the track just extends in a long straight line toward the ball of the foot...way up at the other end. And there, a bit more than halfway along, you can see a line or break where the dirt bunches up just a little. This is characteristic of non-human

primate feet. If this was a person, you probably wouldn't see this line; it doesn't typically exist in humans."

"Oh my goodness," said Mary as Charlie's foot morphology tutorial began to sink in.

"Then we have the ball of the foot, which in this case," said Charlie as he held the tape measure in a transverse fashion, crossing the end of the footprint, "is almost seven inches wide. I defy *any* human walker, runner, scooter or RV invader to have a seven-inch-wide footprint."

"Holy frijolés," said Jorge in a clever rhyme. "By the minute, I'm more glad that I wasn't outside with this thing."

Standing up with some overt groans at the creaking of his joints in the cool air, Charlie suggested, "Jorge, why don't you show me the direction in which you think this creature returned, or retreated, to the woods?"

"I'd be glad to," replied Jorge. "I'm not sure exactly where the thing went, but it was definitely in this direction."

Jorge started walking slowly through the open field toward a stand of large trees bordering the grassy RV parking area. Charlie followed closely behind, scanning the ground carefully. Mary stayed behind at the trailer.

The two men walked up to where the field ended and the trees began. Jorge looked at Charlie and just shrugged his shoulders, as if to indicate the terminus of his knowledge of where the creature might have gone.

"I'll just scope around a bit, then," said Charlie, as if to reply to Jorge's shrug. Charlie stepped into the leafy woods and began examining the lower portions of trees, along with broken branches along the way. He looked for anything resembling a trodden game trail. Despite rooting around for several minutes, he couldn't find anything that indicated the passage of a large creature through this area.

"Well, I guess that's about it," Charlie said to Jorge, who remained standing at the edge of the forest. "Regardless, we've gathered some fine evidence here."

"I'm glad we could be of help," replied Jorge. The men walked side by side back to the parked RV. The day was elapsing and it wasn't getting any warmer out.

As they got to where Mary was standing next to the rig, Charlie offered an in-depth scientific proposition.

"You know, friends, I'm so peckish that I could eat a goose," he said. Both Mary and Jorge laughed at the odd, unexpected turn of phrase. "I noticed that in town there's a nice-looking pub spot that is goose-themed, and likely well-equipped with adult beverages. If you'd like to join me, it'll be my treat!" he said eagerly.

"We won't give you any argument there, Charlie," replied Mary quickly.

Charlie further assessed the situation, saying, "How about if I drive; that way, you don't have to hitch up the pickup again."

"Sure, that'd be fine, Mr. Charlie," said Jorge.

"We can take both of the dogs, and they can wait for us in my rig while we gorge on geese," he added nonsensically.

"Boy, this is sounding like quite the meal we're headed toward," said Mary warily but with a smile.

"Oh, not to worry. I think they have *all kinds* of food," responded Charlie quickly. "It's not just geese and owls and other fowl."

The couple got another laugh at this. Mary went inside the RV to summon Gizzard and Betty, with Jorge locking up once they came out. The five-some then walked across the open field to Charlie's RV and embarked. They'd be heading to little downtown Waupun.

After a brief drive, Motor Myrtle parked in front of a rather faded, dated, single-story eating establishment. Fortunately there were quite a few cars in the lot, which usually indicated either good food or the likelihood of a lottery win at the cash register.

Charlie gave the dogs his "stay" lecture (during which Gizzard looked at him with a highly dubious tilt of the head), locked up the RV, and the three humans headed inside to grab some grub. The setting was a simple bar-and-grill-type arrangement. Charlie had quickly scanned some online reviews asserting that the food and service were excellent here.

Having ordered after being seated, the trio exchanged numerous stories about their travels. Charlie asked Mary and Jorge about their work and family situation, and where they liked to travel for camping and other wilderness experiences. Recent trips they had taken included state parks in the northwestern portion of their home state, Illinois, such as Apple River Canyon and Mississippi Palisades, plus more centralized park locations such as White Pines Forest.

At this point, the female server brought beverages for the diners—iced tea for Mary and Jorge, and a dark stout beer for Charlie.

As was usual in Charlie's experience, the Gutierrez couple had lots of questions for Charlie about his current expedition. Since the kindly pair hailed from the Chicago area, Charlie spent the bulk of his narrative interval describing his recent experiences in Illinois. When he regaled them with the tale about the young female horseback rider from Pawnee, the harrowing chase in which she was involved, and the eventual overnight braiding of her horse's mane, Mary and Jorge expressed amazement at the behavioral complexity and apparent dexterity of the sasquatch creature.

"I've seen things along the way that I never could have predicted," said Charlie in summary, "but that sure keeps things interesting. Oh look, here comes dinner!" he blurted happily.

The female server, assisted by a young man food runner, brought the meals for the trio: a shredded barbecue chicken sandwich with fries for Mary, a loaded "goose burger" (a glorified cheeseburger) and fries for Jorge, and an order of beer-battered cod and shrimp for Charlie.

The hot food was tasty and deeply satisfying, though calorie-heavy. Charlie ended up having a couple—but not too many—beers.

When the group got back into the RV, Betty ran right up to Charlie and essentially accosted him in hopes of scoring some dinner seconds.

"Cod darn-it, Betty!" scolded Charlie as he pushed her paws off of his upper legs. "Now, you just mind your manners, young lady."

Mary and Jorge looked on with interest as Charlie extracted some fried seafood bites for his beagle. Betty wolfed them down instantaneously. Gizzard had sidled right in, not wanting to miss anything. His eyes bugged out and his little tail wagged furiously. An inveterate softie, Charlie couldn't dream of denying the dog a treat. He held up a small fried fishy bite in front of him and looked at Mary and Jorge for the approval needed to corrupt their Shih Tzu.

"Oh, go ahead, I guess," said Mary with an air of slightly annoyed approval.

Like Betty, Gizzard demolished his fish bites with a toothy chomp and was as happy as...a cuddled cod.

Charlie then drove back to the Playful Goose campground to drop Mary, Jorge and Gizzard at their RV. Exiting the vehicle, Mary said they'd be leaving the next day. So, Charlie said his goodbyes to the group—with brief, affectionate shoulder clasps for both Mary and Jorge—and Betty got some parting nuzzles from Gizzard.

"And thank you so much for dinner, Charlie," said Mary.

"Oh of course," he replied. "I deeply appreciate you guys staying the course here and sharing your encounter evidence with me. It's much appreciated. So is the cold beer."

With that, Mary and Jorge laughed and headed to their rig for the night. Charlie drove the short distance over to his pad and the parked Motor Myrtle. He and Betty took a rather dark nighttime walk around the grounds before turning in.

Returning to his documentation work on the computer while still at the campground in Waupun, Charlie saw that he had received a text from Jimmy at the SSDD notifying him of a new witness report that had just come into the database. Apparently, a homeowner living on a rural property in south central Michigan happened upon a line of very large tracks in the early November snow that he couldn't identify. Jimmy asked Charlie if he'd be able to reverse course somewhat and get to the frosty Michigan location in any sort of reasonable interval.

Charlie read the initial account and tentatively scoped out on his map the potential trip route to the location of the observation, in Hillsdale, Michigan. It was not exactly close by. It would require another swing around the bottom of Lake Michigan, and it would be a somewhat frosty visit, certainly. Given the northern latitude and the November timeframe, Charlie wasn't sure about his enthusiasm for a snow-bound investigation, but as usual, he decided to throw caution to the wind. He and his dog would soon be fully up for the adventure. He replied to Jimmy with an all-good-to-go.

Jimmy got right back to him, thanking Charlie for his pluckiness. Jimmy relayed the contact information for the witnesses to Charlie and said he'd let them know that Charlie would soon be on his way. Charlie would plan to call them as he got closer, probably a day or more in the future.

Charlie got changed into his sleeping togs, Betty jumped up onto the bed, and they enjoyed a good night's sleep within the warm confines of Motor Myrtle. As Charlie drifted off, he thought about the proximity of the massive bigfoot that had recently paid a mysterious nighttime call…to his neighbors just a few yards across the lot.

11

A Michigan Monster Makes Its Way

The next monster venture took just a bit more thought than the typical planning required for most investigative sojourns. Unfortunately, south central Michigan was in no way on the way in terms of the direction Charlie and Betty had been traveling. In fact, as the adventurers were about to take up this new challenge, they would have to backtrack south through Milwaukee, pass through Chicago and take I-90 east for some time toward their destination in Hillsdale.

However, Charlie wasn't one to shrink from a new challenge. Well before setting out on the fairly long, circuitous, sometimes cold road trip, he had convinced himself that he was going to maintain a resilient attitude toward whatever unexpected challenge materialized along the way. So, he readily agreed to turn on his dime and head around to Michigan post-haste before the snow melted and the extant track evidence potentially vanished.

Since he had done a couple of snow track investigations previously, Charlie knew that he'd be leaning heavily on his tape measure, camera and snow boots for this one. Warm coats for both himself and his peripatetic pooch pal also would be indicated. He was quite glad that he had stocked up Motor Myrtle with the requisite cold weather gear in advance...just in case.

Getting a very early morning start on a cold, gray day, Myrtle took I-41 south to Milwaukee, transitioning to I-94 east and I-90 east through Chicago. This route took the travelers around the southern tip of the cold, gigantic Lake Michigan and through the very busy windy city of Chicago. Never one of the faster drivers on the road, Charlie got swiftly passed by innumerable big-city commuters in Chicago, some of whom sent less-than-polite looks and gestures in the direction of the elderly rig driver puttering along in the middle lane, with his dog (riding shotgun) apparently giving directions. At least the urban scenery and the massive, adjacent lake were enjoyable to view for Charlie.

Near Chicago, Charlie checked his phone for local eateries. He found a famous Coney Island hot doggery, and stopped in to grab some yummy wieners. At the old, smallish hot dog hangout, he feasted on several dogs with mustard and onions, plus a decadent piece of cream pie for dessert. Betty—back in the RV—reveled in Charlie's return, as he brought a few hot dog leftovers dog-ward.

After Charlie's (and Betty's) meal, Motor Myrtle continued east on I-90, straddling the border between Indiana and Michigan for several hours of driving. The group then took a number of small roads northeast toward Hillsdale.

As the group progressed on their trip (a total of six road hours that day), Charlie began to observe what he expected to see on this travel segment: the appearance of some November snow. Clearly there would be no sunbathing with gamboling geese or luxurious lounging in lawn chairs on this part of the journey. There would, however, be some extra caution exhibited by Charlie as he navigated Myrtle through a more slippery travel landscape.

    Late in the day, Charlie rolled Myrtle to a KOA campground just off South Sand Lake in Hillsdale, where the travelers checked in and claimed their parking pad. Charlie attended to the RV hookups in the cold air. Later, he warmed some frozen burgers in the microwave.

    After dinner, Charlie called the contact number that Jimmy had given him as part of the SSDD report. The contact was Joe Marshall, who owned a home in nearby Osseo where the trackway find occurred just days before. Charlie called and talked with Joe briefly, and they agreed to a meet-up the next day. Joe gave Charlie the address.

    According to Charlie's online research, the large open area to the rear of Mr. Marshall's home was along what was known as the Lost Nations Game Area. Looking deeper into the topography, Charlie saw that the area apparently consisted of hundreds of acres of wooded land with deep creek bottoms and high ridges. Trees in the area were identified as mostly ash and birch, with some stands of pine, plus extensive swamp land. A map Charlie studied showed that the east branch of the St. Joseph River crossed south and west of the property. Snow or no, this investigation location was likely a remote wonderland.

    The next morning in the RV, Charlie and Betty munched on cereal and kibble for breakfast, respectively. Charlie also enjoyed a small orange from a bag he had purchased at their last market stop. Then, following a brief walk around the grounds with Betty (wearing a cute red coat), the investigators headed out to their investigative destination.

After a cautious, unhurried ten-or-so-minute drive on the mostly-cleared roads, Charlie and Betty arrived at Mr. Marshall's rural, tree-encircled single-story home in the late morning. Charlie stopped at the end of the driveway and saw that the home was a low, red-brick-faced building with a pitched, shingled roof. The home had black-shuttered windows and a two-car garage door at one end.

Charlie pulled into the driveway and was pleased to find that it had been recently shoveled or plowed. There were approximately six to seven inches of snow on the ground in most grassy spots, and Mr. Marshall's snow clearing had created snow piles on the sides of the paved driveway about two feet deep. To Charlie, it was starting to look like a lot like winter now.

Motor Myrtle stopped in front of the house's garage door, after which Betty and Charlie stepped out of the RV and took a brief walk around the snow-covered yard, with Betty on leash. She bounced a bit at first as her Southwestern-oriented paws encountered snow for the first time on this trip; a dog coat couldn't warm cold paws.

Soon a man came out from around the back of the house and introduced himself as Joe Marshall.

"I'm pleased to meet you, Joe," said Charlie in his typically polite fashion as he shook the man's hand. Charlie observed that Joe Marshall was a handsome, sturdy gentleman about 45 years old with close-cropped brown hair, wearing khaki hunting-type clothing and heavy boots. To Charlie, he didn't look like someone who spent his weekends in the parlor reading sonnets or playing the piano.

However, despite the need to get better acquainted, Charlie noticed that his constant companion was not taking to the immediate environment.

"You know, Joe," said Charlie, "I'm seeing that my dog Betty here is feeling rather frosty in the cold air and snow. Can you give me a moment while I stow her back in the rig?"

"Oh, sure. There aren't too many animals who like traipsing around out here in the snow," he replied, "with the possible exception of my dog Hogarth. He'd play outside in a tornado."

Charlie laughed and led Betty back to the RV, removing her coat and getting her settled comfortably.

Stepping back down onto the pavement, Charlie got acquainted with Joe.

"So how long have you lived here, Joe?" he asked.

"Well, I guess about 15 years or so," he said. "It's good to be so close to great fishing and hunting and the like. My wife Lisa and I get out a *lot*, and right here is a primo spot for all kinds of wildlife."

"That's excellent," commented Charlie. "Would you like to tell me about some of the…wildlife…you've experienced here most recently?"

"Absolutely, Charlie," replied Joe, "That's why I reported to the SSDD. I figured *someone* might be really interested in the details of what I stumbled over."

The air between the men was quiet for a few slightly awkward seconds.

"Well," resumed Charlie, "would you like to come up into the RV and tell me about your experience?"

"Yeah, I guess that'd be fine," said Joe. "Or we could go in the house if you'd like. Regardless, I'll take you out and show you the snowy grail as soon as you're ready."

Charlie giggled at the Arthurian Holy Grail reference, then Joe followed him up into the RV.

"So this is Betty, huh?" asked Joe, eyeing the dog as she jumped down from a bed to check the man out.

"Yes, she's my travel guide and beagle bombardier," said Charlie.

"Hey there, Betty," said Joe as he snuggled warmly with the intensely tail-wagging dog.

"Let me get my notetaking assistant and I'll be ready for you in a moment," said Charlie to Joe as he pulled out his laptop and set it up on the RV's dining table. "I sure don't want to miss anything, you know."

Joe began his narrative by saying that he had gone out to the back yard one morning several days previous to check on bird feeders when he saw some big, strange tracks crossing the yard at a regular (though expansive) interval.

"As I took in the entire scene," began Joe, "I could see that this was a long set of tracks that initially entered my property on the left side of the yard (as viewed from the back of the house). Then, right behind my house, the tracks turned and headed straight toward the rear of my yard and into the woods."

At the time, walking up and looking more closely at each snowy, deep footprint, Joe realized that these weren't bear tracks, such as left by a big burly mammal that perhaps was late heading for hibernation. The tracks also weren't that of a person on snowshoes, or any other familiar walking creature. According to Joe, to his amazement, these were huge, human, barefoot tracks.

"This was just crazy that this walking individual quite clearly had no shoes on," said Joe to Charlie. "At first it made no sense to me at all. It wasn't until I talked it over with my wife for a while later on that I realized that these could very well be bigfoot tracks."

Joe reported that having had no more snow and no appreciable melt in the past few days, the trackway was still quite distinct. He said that the heel mark, the toe prints, and the way the feet tapered from wide in the front to narrower by the heel were visible on many of the individual (and quite lengthy) foot tracks.

"Once I later realized what I had been looking at, I got a heckuva chill down my spine," reported Joe. "Some sort of giant creature without shoes had walked through my yard recently."

Joe said that his fear spiked with the passing of minutes as the shocking reality sunk in.

He estimated the length of each stride to be at least five feet. Charlie would probably want to tighten up this estimate using his tape measure. The same would go for the measurements of the individual footprints, which Joe estimated to be at least 15 inches long, and approximately six inches across, definitely widening towards the front end of the foot.

Joe said he walked toward the woods next to the footprints, careful not to step over them and degrade them in case someone would want to see them, as Charlie now did.

"Do you think you're ready to check them out, Charlie?"

"You better believe it," replied Charlie without a second's hesitation.

Charlie quickly closed up his laptop, put his coat back on and grabbed his backpack full of investigative gear. He petted Betty briefly then followed Joe out of the RV, closing up securely so Betty wouldn't get overly cold.

Joe walked around the corner toward the rear of his house. About 30 feet behind the house was a wooden bird feeder atop a low pole. Charlie walked up to the feeder behind Joe, who had stopped.

"There they are," said Joe simply.

Charlie observed a line of large impressions in the snow that traversed the yard from left to right, coming right up to the bird feeder. All of the impressions leading into the yard seemed clear at first observance, but as the tracks reached the area of the bird feeder, they became muddled and messy. Clearly something had stood at this spot and meandered about just a bit, blurring the footprints.

Charlie stepped back to more closely observe the clear part of the trackway. The individual prints looked quite far apart— definitely not in the human range of stride at first blush.

Extracting his tape measure from his backpack (along with his camera that he had stowed this time due to the cold), Charlie carefully walked up to the first very clear footprint, knelt down, extended the yellow tape and promptly measured the track at 16.5 inches in length. He stood up and took a picture of the track. He then spread the tape out much further between the first and next track, and he found that the stride length was just over six feet. He took another picture, plus photos of the stride without the tape measure.

"These prints are still remarkably clear, Joe," said Charlie enthusiastically. "I'm *so* glad you reported your find to the SSDD."

"I just figured this was unusual enough that it should probably be documented for the record," replied Joe thoughtfully.

Charlie had a lot of experience studying sasquatch tracks in many ground conditions, from snow to mud to dust to flattened trail foliage. When he knelt down and very closely examined the tracks, he realized that many of them showed slight evidence of the mid-tarsal break common to sasquatch foot evidence. In snowy conditions, the distinctive evidence of a mid-tarsal break appears as a compression of snow into a thin lateral line or lump across the middle of the foot track.

Still kneeling in the snow, Charlie took some additional, very close-up photographs, some showing the undisputable tape measure evidence of both the individual track lengths and the overall stride length. Joe stayed out of the way and watched him.

Standing up and stepping back, Charlie turned to his right and observed the direction of the tracks as they headed away from the house and back into the woods.

"We should probably follow those tracks, wouldn't you say, young man?" said Charlie briskly.

Joe was quiet for quite a few seconds, then appeared to get ahold of his seeming hesitancy about tracking a possibly huge creature.

"Well sure, I guess we can do that, but know that my wife Lisa will have soup and sandwiches ready for us before long," he said.

Laughing somewhat, Charlie said, "Soup and sandwiches? Spectacular! But please don't worry about this creature, Joe. I'm certain that it's as far away as a walk on a warm beach by now."

So, still avoiding ruining any of the snowy tracks by stomping gracelessly on them, Charlie and Joe gingerly walked parallel to the track line and followed it into the woods. The trees at this time of year, many 50 to 80 feet tall, were almost entirely bare. The sky was gray and non-cheerful. Charlie continued taking photos of the track line and the overall area as the men walked between the big trees. It was quite cold.

After a couple minutes of slow and deliberate walking, the two men found that the tracks led to a ridge that dropped almost straight down nearly 70 feet to a creek bottom. Whatever made the tracks had walked straight down the steep grade...in the snow.

Charlie and Joe attempted to follow the tracks down the ridge, but both men frequently lost their traction, slipped, fell over, and slid downward a bit on their backsides. Conversely, the creature's tracks were pristine and did not appear to slip at all as they proceeded straight down the steep ridge unimpeded.

It took the men quite a few minutes to clumsily descend the slippery slope. Charlie tried taking a few photos of the footprints as they descended.

"This is one of those things that I'm probably way too old for," said Charlie to Joe as the men struggled mightily to keep their feet amidst the descent.

"Yeah, me too, actually" agreed Joe.

Once finally at the bottom of the hill, Charlie observed multiple deer and coyote tracks mixed in with the much larger bigfoot tracks, but it was clear that nothing else had walked up or down the ridge other than the large bipedal creature (and now the two small bipedal creatures). The foot traffic appeared rather heavy in this area, and the abundant, jumbled tracks seemed to head mostly out toward the large St. Joseph River at this lower elevation.

Summarizing somewhat, Joe said that he doubted that any human could have steadily traveled the steep, slippery slope all the way down to the low, distant creek bed. Charlie agreed with that, and added that few human winter walkers have a 16-inch track and a 6-foot stride length.

Having paced several hundred yards into the woods, all the way to the bottom of the steep ridge, Charlie and Joe talked about potentially heading back to the (likely warm) house.

However, while still standing within the snow-covered creek bed amidst the trees, just before heading back, Charlie stood very still and scanned slowly across and through the trees. He looked far out across the nearby (apparently) frozen, snow-covered river. Suddenly, quite distant on the other side of the river, Charlie spotted a dark figure on the riverbank in front of a large stand of trees. The figure was exceedingly far away, but in Charlie's sight, it was all one dark color and likely not a person.

"You know, I see a very dark, human-shaped figure across the river right now," Charlie said to Joe, "but I don't think it's a typical human."

Joe thought about this new development for a moment and said, "Who knows? That may be our big boy."

Charlie got his camera pulled up into position and tried to use the zoom lens to target the creature and take some extremely long-distance snaps. However, it was quite difficult to get a clear view given the distance to the figure, which soon walked up the hill beyond the river bank and into the woods. The big trees in Charlie's foreground made any sort of clear visual documentation impossible.

"Well, Joe, I'm not sure how to proceed at this point," admitted Charlie to his excursion pal. Joe didn't offer any suggestions toward one course of action or another.

Charlie just stood in place and took several fairly agonizing, quiet minutes trying to decide whether to pursue the distant (and now not visible) individual or not. Such opportunities were obviously quite rare, after all. However, by his own calculus, given his age, physical condition, the late time of day, the uncertain ice depth on the river and the quite frigid weather conditions at present, he ultimately decided to remain on this side of the river and be satisfied with the trackway evidence he had already gathered. It was quite a painful call to make, although probably prudent.

Charlie had taken several fairly futile photo attempts to capture the image of the small black moving dot in the distance before it disappeared into the woods. He was quite certain that these shots  would join the unimpressive though well populated pantheon of "blob-squatch" pictures people had taken over the years…when they were too far away or otherwise unprepared to catch meaningful visual evidence.

So, at this point Charlie needed to gain some quick perspective on his situation. He reminded himself that he had gathered ample evidence at the trackway site—an in-person witness interview, close observation of footprint morphology, extensive photographic scale evidence of track and stride length, and an overall estimation of the length of the full trackway through the woods. The SSDD would be fortunate to reel in such a treasure trove of bigfoot evidence.

"Uh, I suppose we should head back, Joe. It looks like I've gotten all I can get today," said Charlie in a somewhat disappointed tone to the homeowner.

"Okay, Charlie," said Joe, "Besides, it's getting *dang* cold out here."

With that, the two men strove to retrace (in reverse) the steps that they had taken down the tall ridge. As with the descent, the ascent encompassed several slips, falls and utterances of decidedly blue language. Charlie got positively worn out ascending the 70-or-so-foot-tall slippery ridge.

At one point, having fallen onto his fanny, Charlie said with mild exasperation, "Joe, don't you think it would be better if I came back in the summer and joined you for a jump in the river? I can do an excellent fat-guy cannonball."

Joe chuckled and extended a hand to Charlie to help him to his feet.

"You know, this place is just beautiful in the summer," said Joe, "and you don't hit the ground nearly as much...unless you drop your beer or your weed."

Charlie appreciated Joe's reference to the summer salves of adult indulgence.

The two men continued their cold, stalwart trek back to the house, which became a much more comfortable walk once they had cleared the high ridge.

Getting back to the house, Joe invited Charlie inside. Charlie said that, first, however, he'd need to check on his quadrupedal overseer, Betty.

"Oh heck, bring her in, Charlie," said Joe. "Hogarth will probably like her a lot, but not as a meal...necessarily."

Appreciatively, Charlie walked over to the RV and returned with Betty on leash.

Entering a back door of the house, Joe and Charlie stood in a narrow laundry room and gradually shed their heavy coats, boots and gear. Beneath a small window facing the back yard, Charlie generated a healthy pile of clothing and backpack contents, flopping it all atop a white clothes dryer. As Charlie let Betty off her leash, she did a robust, twisting head shake now that she was untethered and comfortably in from the snow and cold.

Seconds later, a flash of black and white burst into the small, dark room from another portion of the house. It apparently was Joe's dog, an Australian shepherd mix, who instantly crashed into Betty as part of an over-enthusiastic greeting.

"Hogarth, you crazy thing," said Joe affectionately. "Go easy on Betty here."

With bright, keen eyes, a mostly black coat, long legs and a docked (i.e., nonexistent) tail, the dog clearly dwarfed Betty and essentially smothered her with introductory affection.

Now petting the dog robustly about the head and back, Charlie asked Joe, "So how did you arrive on the name Hogarth for this big bundle of energy?"

Joe laughed a bit and explained. "A bunch of years ago there was a great animated movie, 'The Iron Giant,' whose main character was a kindly, adventurous boy, Hogarth. It's an *extremely* silly name and we thought it fit this wacky fur ball here."

"Well, I'd be inclined to agree with you on the fitting appellation," said Charlie articulately.

The two humans and two canines headed together into a large kitchen directly off the laundry room.

"Hi sweetie, we survived," said Joe wearily to a comely brunette of medium height. Standing with her back to the kitchen sink, the woman was wearing a bright green cotton long-sleeve shirt atop blue jeans, with heavy, fluffy winter slippers beneath.

"Charlie, this is my wife, Lisa. Lisa, this is Charlie Marlowe, the investigator I told you about," said Joe.

The two newly introduced people now stepped toward each other and shook hands in front of the kitchen table.

"It's quite lovely to meet you, Lisa," said Charlie in his customarily hyper-polite fashion as he shook Lisa's hand affectionately and bowed down slightly.

"It's nice to meet you too, Charlie," said Lisa. "Is there any reason at all why you'd want to stumble around out there in the snow and wind?"

Charlie stifled a mild giggle and replied, "Well, I'll admit that it's somewhat of a chronic neurosis of mine—chasing fleeting evidence of overgrown great apes through forbidding territories and truly subpar weather. I believe there's a psychiatric diagnosis for that somewhere in a very fat medical book."

Lisa and Joe both got a good laugh over this self-deprecating description.

"Well, since you apparently pulled through," began Lisa, "you're welcome to join us for some minestrone soup and grilled cheese sandwiches."

As usual, Charlie hesitated less than would a fly at a summer barbecue.

"Minestrone and a sandwich—that sounds like manna from heaven to me at this juncture," said Charlie enthusiastically.

On a stove underneath an aluminum exhaust cover, the red soup in a large silver pot was already heated up and bubbling audibly. Joe began to help Lisa with preparing the sandwiches. He pulled the bread out of a cylindrical metal breadbox, Lisa pulled cheese and butter from the refrigerator, and the couple got to work on sandwich construction.

Lisa asked questions of Charlie as she worked. "So, what did you think of those wild footprints out there?"

"I thought they were entirely impressive," Charlie replied. "I doubt Joe has had a chance to tell you yet, but we measured them at more than 16 inches in length each."

"That is one big foot!" was Lisa's on-target reply.

"Yes, and it was great that there had been no additional snow, rain or clumsy walkers to degrade the prints out there," added Charlie. "I got excellent photos with outstanding foot detail—both of the many individual prints and the full trackway in scale. The prints were six feet apart."

"Whoa, that's a hefty snow strider," agreed Lisa. She looked at Charlie for a few moments, then stepped demonstratively forward with one foot, achieving about a three and a half foot stride in the milieu of the cozy kitchen.

"You'll *never* make it as a bigfoot," said Joe in response.

"So," replied Lisa, "you're telling me to keep my day job?"

"Yes, honey, you're an experienced accountant, and I don't think monster moves are in your vocational future, unfortunately."

The entire trio laughed heartily at this gleeful repartee.

Just then, a rampantly unsupervised Hogarth burst into the kitchen from the laundry room and ran right up to Charlie. Looking intently at the male visitor, Hogarth had one of Charlie's boots in his mouth, with heavy laces hanging down to the floor like a scraggly beard.

Before Charlie could say a thing, Hogarth quickly lowered his chin to the floor, with his haunches held up high in back, and looked at Charlie with sparkling eyes and a deeply mischievous countenance.

As Charlie reached toward Hogarth with one hand, the dog burst forth from his position and ran through and out of the kitchen, opposite the laundry room. He carried the boot like a holy relic.

Lisa shouted, "Hogarth, bring that back!"

The dog clearly had other ideas, as the trio of humans could hear him pounding down hallways and into rooms elsewhere, gleefully toting his new treasure.

Lisa spoke again. "Joe, *please* go lasso that crazy goof and get this man's footwear back."

Charlie just shook his head in amazement at the scofflaw dog's boot burglary.

"I believe he's got quite the mind of his own," said Charlie.

"You can't *begin* to imagine," said Joe as he hurried out of the room in pursuit of the kleptomanic canine.

Soon, Charlie and Lisa heard Hogarth physically crash into Betty again, likely in the living room or some other large space beyond. There was a clear rumble and tumble that only the dogs could generate, while Betty yipped once with an edge of annoyed defensiveness.

"Come on now, Hogarth!" said Joe from the other room, still apparently pursuing the crazy quadruped.

Back in the kitchen, Lisa had microwaved some strips of bacon and was sprinkling the crumbles into the cheese sandwiches before grilling them on a griddle.

Charlie deeply approved of this delectable development.

Soon Joe returned with the burgled boot. "That dog is a major loon," he said as he handed the boot back to Charlie. Charlie walked over to the laundry room and returned with his *other* boot, putting them both back on and tying the laces for purposes of preserving possession. Hogarth stood at the entrance to the kitchen, wagging his butt at the proceedings, ready to foment more mischief if possible.

Before long the grub was ready, so the three adults sat together at the kitchen table and enjoyed some winter comfort food—temporarily without the infusion of over-whacked dog energy. Regardless, Charlie loved the tomato, pasta and vegetable soup in addition to the tasty tendrils of cheese that gushed from the grilled sandwiches. Ah, gastronomic bliss on a cold day.

As they ate, the trio discussed more bigfoot topics.

"So where else have you been on your trip?" asked Lisa thoughtfully.

Charlie paused to consider the rounds that he and his dog had made recently. He swallowed a bite of warm sandwich and looked up toward the ceiling in contemplation, then fashioned a piecemeal reply.

"Well, let's see. We encountered evidence of a 500-pound pumpkin 'squatch in Oklahoma...a snake-tossing bigfoot in Texas...a four-foot-tall monster youngster in Florida...a colossal, hairy brute charging out of a swamp in Pennsylvania...and an Illinois sasquatch that chased a horse then braided its mane later. And then some. Did you get all that?!" asked Charlie finally with a knowing laugh.

"Jeepers, you *have* been out on the trail, haven't you?!" exclaimed Lisa.

"Yeah, there are always surprises out there, wherever you go looking for these creatures," replied Charlie. "I've learned and have seen a lot...so far. We've got a ways to go yet."

Just as Charlie said that, Betty came charging into the kitchen with Hogarth in close pursuit. The big dog was carrying in his mouth an enormous pine cone that must have served as a decoration in some other sector of the house. Following after Betty, he careened around the corner of the table, slipped on a throw rug and crashed with a thud into the dishwasher. He dropped the pine cone, which spun aimlessly across the linoleum. The kitchen proceedings were beginning to sound like a demolition derby.

"Hogarth, take it *easy*!" urged Joe as the manic dog reversed and tore out of the kitchen in pursuit of Betty, who had nimbly squirmed between the human legs under the kitchen table and escaped back out of the room, her claws churning like a speedy water wheel on a dry surface.

"These two are having just way too much fun, I think," said Lisa.

"Well, there's always a way to get their attention," said Charlie. He ripped off a corner of his sandwich. "Betty, I've got some grilled cheese for you!" he cried in a sing-song voice. He also emitted a two-note high-pitched whistle. The dog instantly returned the kitchen, sidled up to Charlie and got her sliver of sandwich. It was gone in less than half a second. Hogarth looked on with overt jealousy.

Once things settled down a bit and the people finished their meal and their cleanup, Joe asked Charlie if he and the dog had a place to stay tonight. The evening outside was pitch black by this time.

Charlie described his arrangements at the nearby RV park. "We're lucky that it hasn't snowed anymore, so getting back to the KOA should be pretty easy," he added.

The group chatted some more, and soon Charlie said his goodbyes to everyone, thanking Joe for sharing the trackway evidence and expressing gratitude to Lisa for her hospitality. Of course, Charlie also gave Hogarth generous hugs and belly rubs before walking Betty back out to the RV.

"I don't think someone here's going to be too happy that you're leaving," said Joe of his highly spirited pooch as Charlie and Betty walked across the cold driveway.

"He sure is a good boy, though awfully energetic," shouted Charlie finally to Joe and Lisa at the back door. "Take good care of your mom and dad, Hogarth!" The dog looked longingly at the departing guests, his tiny tail nubbin still going a mile a minute.

Joe had turned on a bright light above the garage to illuminate the travelers' egress, but the spot didn't cut through any of the bleak cold that gripped the environment.

Charlie said, "*Oy*, it's cold out here, wouldn't you say, Betty?" as the duo climbed up into the RV.

After firing up and warming Motor Myrtle, Charlie made the short drive back to the camping area and got the hookups in place for the night. He was very glad to finish up that frigid task and get back inside the big, warming vehicle for the night.

Before it got too late, Charlie wrestled Betty into her coat and took her for a brief, cold walk around the campground. They both scooted quickly and thankfully back into the RV afterward.

Later, working on his laptop to fully enter all the evidence he had gathered that day, Charlie looked over his recent texts, calls and emails to see if anything was shaking in the realm of bigfoot sightings. He spotted a text from an old SSDD colleague of his, Bill Bennett, from Missouri. Bill reported that an unusual occurrence had transpired near the town of Prairie Home, MO needing investigative attention. Was Charlie available to take a look?

Charlie texted back to Bill in the affirmative. Missouri was quite a bit southwest of Charlie's current location, and at this late juncture of the year might prove considerably more comfortable than Michigan. Taking this "job" also would get Charlie, Betty and Myrtle one major step closer to home...and Francesca.

So, before calling it yet another eventful day, Charlie decided that he was seriously missing his love and would really enjoy hearing her voice. He looked at the clock and, despite the lateness of the hour here, realized that Francesca was two hours behind him in Santa Fe and wouldn't likely object to receiving a call at this point.

"How are you doing, honey?" he asked lovingly after Francesca picked up.

"Do I know you, sir? Can you show me some ID?" she asked flippantly.

"I promise that we're married," replied Charlie, "and that we've done glamorous chores together in the garage."

"Oh, well, in that case, at least the honeymoon isn't over yet," said Francesca.

The distant spouses talked long, lovingly and laughingly, zinging each other with friendly verbal barbs.

Amidst the mirth, Charlie explained where Myrtle was situated currently, and where they were likely off to next.

"So, how cold is it in Michigan in November?" asked Francesca.

"Well, I think Frosty the Snow Beast would be very happy here," explained Charlie, "but Betty and I have pretty much gotten our fat fannies frozen."

"And speaking of frosty dogs," he continued, "We've been meeting lots of hyper-energetic pooches along the way, I must say. Here in Michigan, we spent time with an Australian shepherd mix who charged around so much that he nearly ground Betty's legs down to nubs."

Francesca got a good laugh at this puppy playtime perspective.

"But anyway, this is the last of the northern destinations that I know of," said Charlie, explaining the plans for their subsequent Missouri destination. "It looks like we'll soon be turning south and heading back toward the high desert."

"You say 'it looks like,'" said Francesca. "Does that mean there's more chance of that than your cleaning the bathroom anytime soon?" she asked with a friendly bite.

"We're definitely coming into the home stretch, honey, I promise."

Soon Charlie and Betty were tucked into bed in the RV, enjoying an extra blanket on this cold, dark night. Before dropping off to sleep, Charlie let himself imagine enjoying the loving comfort of being with Francesca again soon, although not necessarily doing "glamorous" chores in the garage.

12

JUST SPOOLING AROUND

Although Charlie greatly approved of the southwest direction that the crew would be taking on this next segment of the trip, it was not going to be swift sailing. There were quite a few miles to cover.

Motor Myrtle headed out of camp early in the morning, and Charlie stopped to grab a fast food breakfast before rolling out of town. The group picked up I-69 south and eventually passed Fort Wayne, Indiana. Continuing south, they stopped in Indianapolis for a late lunch, as they had prior to their visit in Pawnee, Illinois. In fact, Myrtle stopped at the same hip microbrew pub they had visited previously. However, instead of ordering chicken and biscuits this time, Charlie had a blackened shrimp po' boy sandwich and an amber beer. The nearly-bulging Betty got a couple of shrimp bites in her beagle bag.

Leaving Indy, the group picked up I-70 west and stayed on that highway all the way through St. Louis, arriving in the big city in the evening after about eight hours on the road. Given the full day of driving, Charlie felt fully fatigued and decided to stop in St. Louis to restock the RV supplies and get some rest. On West Florissant Avenue in St. Louis, a super-sized Walmart (and its parking lot) provided ample provisions and overnight parking. One of the supply items Charlie wanted to replenish was plaster of paris so that he could fashion additional track casts if indicated.

The next morning, after taking Betty for a walk around the huge parking lot, Charlie steered Motor Myrtle over to a local Krispy Kreme doughnut shop to commit some early a.m. caloric crimes before departing town. This time, he spared Betty the sweet, fatty food. The group continued west on I-70 for about two hours. Then, somewhere near the town of Columbia, Charlie pulled over to call the next witness and confirm their meeting arrangements. Charlie talked with Gene Mayer, the homeowner whom he'd be visiting. The morning had elapsed, so Charlie agreed to come straight to Gene's house instead of stopping elsewhere first. Gene gave him the local directions.

To finish up their highway driving on this leg of the trip, the group exited I-70 and picked up Missouri Route 87 south to their destination, Prairie Home. It was a cloudy November day, but not too cold, by Charlie's reckoning. This was a nice change.

As Motor Myrtle arrived in front of Gene Mayer's address, Charlie observed a low, white, one-story rancher-type home atop a small bluff. Some trees and brush surrounded the house. An abundance of quite large trees (both conifer and leafy) stood tall behind the home.

Although the homes in this area didn't appear luxurious, the lot sizes seemed quite generous; no houses were close together. Charlie made a left turn into the long driveway, and parked close to Mr. Mayer's house. The entire front of the house had a long, large roof overhang that would likely make resting in a rocker atop this hill quite pleasant.

Charlie walked along the covered porch to the front door of the home and rang the bell. An average-sized man in his late 50s or early 60s (by Charlie's estimation) opened the door. He wore glasses and an old blue work shirt. Charlie introduced himself, and so did Gene. They shook hands, and Gene invited Charlie inside.

The two men walked a short distance to the house's living room to discuss Gene's apparent creature experience.

"Sit anywhere you'd like, Charlie," said Gene.

"Thank you. You have a lovely home."

"Thanks, but that's mostly my wife Rebecca's doing," replied Gene. "She's got a nice touch with decorating and with plants. I've got a nice touch with sawing things in half and cleaning fish."

Charlie found this self-assessment an amusing study in companion comportment contrasts.

"Can I get you some water or coffee?" asked Gene politely.

"Uh, I guess some water would be nice."

Gene left the room and quickly returned with a tall glass of ice water for Charlie. Gene appeared to have gotten some sort of non-cola soda drink.

"Thank you, Gene, why don't you tell me about your… experiences…here," suggested Charlie as he set up his laptop and began taking notes.

"Well, as you might have noticed on your way in," began Gene, "our property backs up to quite an expanse of forest. Sprinkled throughout the area are lots of family farms, but not much commercial activity right in this area. There are also quite a few wildlife conservation areas nearby. So, it's not uncommon to see all kinds of animals roll through here—deer, wild turkey, prairie chicken, geese, foxes, bobcats, raccoons—the whole gamut. We're used to seeing all of it—in the woods, out on the trails and right up to the house. But what showed up lately...isn't your typical Prairie Home wildlife, I don't think."

Charlie began to get the gist of Gene's narrative quite quickly.

"Anyway, I used to work for the phone company. So a few years ago I had an idea, and asked a buddy who still worked at the company to bring me one of those big old wooden cable spools that wasn't being used any longer. He drove it out here along with a pal in his F-350 pickup one day. It took three of us to wrestle  this thing out of the truck bed and roll it around to the back yard. It weighed a damn ton. My intention was to use it as a permanent picnic table out back. We got it to where I wanted it near a tree, flipped it on its side, and voila—instant picnic table. Not long after, I put a set of deck chairs around the table, which was 20 or 25 feet behind the house. It was a pretty nice setup, I guess."

"Oh, and don't worry, Charlie," added Gene with a bit of a laugh. "The main thrust of this story isn't backyard furniture."

Charlie found this comment amusing, but didn't yet know where Gene would take this narrative.

"So, one morning I came out back and noticed right away that my cable spool table was gone. This was a pretty big surprise to me, as the spool was super heavy and would have taken some serious organization and manpower to drag it off the property. I quickly got mad at whoever did this."

Gene described doing a bit of investigation to try and figure out what had happened. "The picnic chairs were knocked over and scattered all around. As I was scanning the area, I looked at this slightly worn path through the grass that led from my property to the edge of the forest. I decided to follow the path to see if there was evidence of the cable spool having been moved in that direction."

"Sure enough, I could see places on the path where it looked like the spool had been rolled (looking like parallel wagon wheel tracks), but also places where it must have actually been picked up and carried or something. I also spotted a few very large, human-like footprints on the path. The footprints looked particularly deep in the dirt where I couldn't find any signs of the spool rolling—I guess suggesting that this big chunk of wood had been picked up and carried at these spots."

"Goodness, me," replied Charlie with an expanding amount of amazement.

Gene continued his account. "And you know, an odd thing about the path evidence was that I couldn't see any prints of a bunch of guys' shoes or boots—only these big, barefooted tracks. Plus, there wasn't more than the one set of footprints—meaning that a single…person…carried or rolled the spool. Who on earth could have done that?"

Gene reported that he had continued to follow the trail containing the trackway and cable spool markings. To his great surprise, the evidence continued onward for more than a mile across variegated and quite rugged terrain including gullies, streams, ridges and lots of deadfall from the adjacent tree line.

That day, several weeks before, Gene apparently followed the trail and trackway for as long as he had the time to spare, but then had to turn around and head home before darkness fell. He never did find the big wooden spool.

While walking home that day, pondering the possibilities, Gene decided that the spool table was much too heavy for youngsters or teens to have taken as a prank, particularly because of the distance across which the spool was apparently steered and carried. However, there was no evidence at all of equipment having been used in the theft. Gene considered this quite a mystery indeed.

"I can see how you had quite a conundrum on your hands there, Gene," said Charlie in response to the man's unusual account.

"You betcha...and the more I thought about it, the more it sort of bugged me that someone could have done all this by themselves. What's the motivation, and how did they get it done?" he asked rhetorically.

"I certainly haven't a clue," said Charlie. He hesitated for several moments. "Can you show me the area where this happened?"

"Well yeah, it's just right out the back door here," said Gene. He stood up and went to a hallway closet to get his coat. "It's a bit chilly out there, you know," said Gene in a helpful tone, to his guests.

"Oh yes, you're right," replied Charlie. He put his own overcoat back on and slipped Betty into her red coat. He also had his backpack at the ready, having stowed the laptop inside.

Gene led his guests through the house to a back door. Before arriving there, they came upon Gene's wife seated at a table in a large work room.

"This is my wife Rebecca," said Gene, "and this is Charlie Marlowe the investigator, and his dog Betty."

A pretty woman of about Gene's age, with red hair transitioning to gray, very fair skin, and wearing an off-white turtleneck sweater, greeted Charlie kindly from behind the table. He walked up to her and extended his right hand across the table.

She stood up and said in a soft voice, "It's a pleasure to meet you, Charlie, welcome to our home," shaking hands with Charlie.

"The pleasure is all mine, Rebecca," said Charlie, offering his usual introductory smile and hyper-polite bow. "Are you an artist?" he inquired as he observed her work area.

"Right now I'm making wildlife lap blankets," she replied with an emerging smile, "...but they're intended for people, not wildlife." Charlie giggled at her craft description.

"Uh, Becca," said Gene, "we're going to go out and look at what's left of our picnic area, and maybe follow the trail some. We might scope around a bit, and I'm not sure exactly when we'll be back. If you get attacked by any pizza delivery dudes, please relieve him of one or two of his pies," said Gene, clearly suggesting that a meal for the guests might be indicated later.

"I get it, Gene," said Rebecca with a smile.

With Gene taking the lead, the investigative group then exited the back door to look around.

Walking just a few feet outdoors into the cloudy, cool day, the group took stock of the now-ruined picnic area just behind the house.

Gene showed Charlie where the table had sat amidst the lawn chairs. A large flattened circle of what used to be grass was clearly visible where the heavy, tipped over spool had resided for a couple of years. Several chairs still lay askew on the ground.

"So, this is the crime scene?" said Charlie to Gene.

"Uh huh, but this is just the beginning. Let me show you this trail or trackway or whatever."

Gene led Charlie and Betty to a thin, worn dirt trail. The group left Gene's property on this trail and followed the evidence markings leading to the woods. Here, Charlie got his first look at the parallel spool tracks.

At one point where there was no spool marking on the ground, Charlie spotted a rather clear footprint in the dried mud. He got out his tape measure and camera to document the impressive find. The footprint was just over 18 inches long and 6.75 inches wide at the ball of the foot. Fairly clear digit impressions were visible in the dirt, with the footprint being about two inches deep. Charlie took pictures from various angles.

He said to Gene, "You can see from this track that your cable table thief was clearly a sizeable perp."

"Eighteen inches long?" asked Gene in an incredulous tone, to no one in particular.

Next, the trio continued their walk along evidence row. Every once in a while, Gene would point out where the spool had left impressions in the dirt and weeds. With the spool tracks not being all that numerous, Charlie theorized that the big wooden spool had been carried more than rolled. This was an incredible realization.

Gene, Charlie and Betty hiked along the trail for some time. It was pretty easy to follow, as the occasional huge footprint marks and parallel spool tracks were rather unmistakable. Plus the trail appeared to have been in use for a long time—likely a well-traveled animal pathway that proceeded cleanly between the trees and wasn't obstructed by any particularly imposing trail breaks or obstructions. To continue to follow the trail, the group did have to cross a couple of small streams and also a few steep gullies requiring particular caution. These minor impediments brought to mind for Charlie the impressive feat that the creature's carrying of the spool represented.

Then something different occurred. After rounding a small corner in the trail, the group came upon a very large tree lying across the trail and extending a good 30 perpendicular feet out from the edges of each side of the trail. What was once a tall, thick tree was now a very effective trail block.

Looking down quizzically at the felled tree, Gene scratched behind an ear and said, "You know, this tree wasn't across here a few weeks ago."

Charlie's interest in this new obstacle began to grow. He walked off the trail and over to where the trunk of the tree had broken off. He examined the light-colored wood that previously constituted the core of the tree. The tree break was approximately three to four feet high, with large, splintered shards of shredded wood sticking out vertically and horizontally. The remainder of the tree, fully intact, headed toward and crossed the trail. There was no sign of tools, equipment or even the burn mark of a lightning strike to indicate why the tree had come down. Charlie, of course, had a theory.

He said to Gene, "There's a good chance this tree had some serious help coming down."

Gene had no idea what Charlie was talking about. Charlie noticed Gene's blank expression and realized that he didn't grasp the import of this forest marker.

Charlie went back to being an educator. "This tree is not in any way unhealthy, Gene. Look closely; it's fresh and vibrant from bottom to top. There's no natural reason for it to have come down. It's too healthy to have been felled by wind, and the roots weren't pulled up. There are no marks of cutting tools. You can see that there wasn't a lightning strike here. It's likely that this tree was simply placed here by our big, strong friend as a 'stay out' indicator to humans and other potential intruders. I don't think he wanted anyone crossing into this zone."

Gene stood with hands on hips pondering what may have happened at this spot. "I can't believe it. Something could just break a tree that big and bring it down?"

"Yes," replied Charlie, "something that can carry a huge spool could also probably fell a tree."

"Oh my goodness," was all that Gene could say.

Charlie reached for his camera and took a few pictures, both of the splintered tree break and the effective blockage of the trail.

Before long, the group resumed their slow walking pace after they climbed over the trail "gate." (Betty walked underneath.) Charlie continued to stop and look at every visible type of track along the way. Finally, after more than a mile of careful walking and observation—beyond the point where Gene indicated he had truncated his initial evidence search—the trio came to the edge of a very steep gulley with bare earth walls leading down to a natural drainage.

Looking down and scanning the whole area, Charlie said, "Gene, I think that may be your wayward furniture over there."

Gene's eyes widened as he spotted the large, light brown cylindrical object lying crookedly at the bottom of the ditch about 75 feet from where the investigating party stood.

"I, uh, I can't believe it!" exclaimed Gene in a stuttering fashion to Charlie and Betty. "Whatever moved that spool way out here and tossed it into the gulch must have been the most powerful thing walking this planet."

Although he said nothing in reply this time, Charlie was in full agreement with Gene's assessment. All was quiet for several moments before Gene piped up again.

"And *why the heck did someone need to take my cable table?!*" he yelled with overt annoyance, seemingly to the spool itself, clumsily shipwrecked across the way at the bottom of the large ditch.

At this very moment Betty started to growl. She was looking to her left, ahead of the group, along the top left edge of the gulley.

Charlie said, "What's the matter, girl?" He bent down to grab ahold of her.

She continued to growl and was now straining at her leash, trying to run in the direction of whatever it was she had spotted or heard.

Charlie looked in that direction and was stunned to see someone standing at the edge of the trees watching the group, on the same side of the chasm as them. This person was immensely tall and covered with flowing dark hair. Charlie knew immediately what he was looking at, about 200 feet away. It had a large, conical head placed closely upon gigantically wide shoulders, with a near-human expression on a face that was lighter in color than the rest of the creature, massively long arms and legs that were full of muscles, and huge hands hanging far down to the side of its legs.

Charlie whispered insistently to the others, "Um, I believe that's our spool culprit over there, my friends."

While Charlie was bent down trying to calm Betty, yet still eyeing up the sasquatch, an instantly flabbergasted Gene nearly lost his footing and fell over into the ditch as soon as he took in the incredible sight.

"Oh my *God*!" was all he could say, rather quietly.

"Um, Gene, would you mind holding onto Miss Betty for a moment?" Charlie whispered with urgency.

Gene did not reply quickly.

"Oh, yeah, sure," he eventually stammered to Charlie as he tried to recover from overwhelming shock. He took Betty's leash while continuing to look at the immense creature. Meanwhile Betty issued several aggressive barks in the creature's direction.

Astoundingly, the creature essentially answered Betty's salvo, sending a massive, angry, staccato grunt into the air and right through the permeable bodies of the comparatively tiny, helpless witnesses at which he was now staring threateningly. The sound echoed deeply throughout the forest.

"Oh Lord Jesus," said Gene in reaction to the creature's warning vocalization. "I think I'm gonna be sick." The man now seemed to have been propelled out to the very edge of consciousness.

"Uh, yeah, he's not real happy," exhaled Charlie to the others, shaking his head forcefully in an attempt to recover from the monster's low infrasound blast. As anyone knew who had ever encountered such a devastating sound out in nature, recovery was never an easy task. Charlie reached down and began feebly fumbling with his camera in an attempt to get a photo.

However, the creature wasn't done with the investigative party just yet. The insanely tall beast took one huge step forward toward the humans and dog, and then stretched out its legs in a full-speed, all-out running charge toward them.

The creature issued another rapid huff as it closed in on the group with utterly frightening speed, its feet producing gargantuan thuds that rippled through the area. All three helpless beings were suddenly fairly certain that death was upon them. The creature was titanically muscular, full of anger, and brimming with absolute locomotive power. With long hair flying behind its body at full speed, the creature was unequivocally homicidal. It would be upon the group in seconds to extinguish their lives.

Eyes hugely widened at the terrifying sight, Gene said something that sounded like "Whatduhmumma," then he lost his footing, collapsed and began rolling down the steep slope of the gulley in the dirt. Charlie dropped to his knees on the ground, clutching at Betty for dear life.

Arms swinging and pounding with energy, the creature got within about fifteen feet of the group, then stopped and looked angrily down at them—gigantic dark hands balled into massive fists that he held out at arm's length. So close to the bigfoot now, Charlie instantly became overwhelmed by a foul, garbage-like smell. He rolled down onto his side, protectively clutching his now inert dog.

Fortunately, before reaching the humans and dog, the massive creature turned promptly around and began walking back in the direction from which it had come. It had produced the desired effect. Issuing huge, seemingly angry footfalls, the creature walked with long strides along the top edge of the gulley until it got to the trees and the spot where it had exited the forest. Turning and looking back once at the people, the creature then walked belligerently back into the trees, knocking aside forest growth of all sizes as it strode.

The prominent sasquatch sounds got quiet quickly as the creature exited the area; he seemed to be making good time in his leave-taking from the investigating group. Soon, the heavy, leafy footsteps had dissipated and stopped altogether. To the extent they were conscious, the humans remaining weren't displeased by this development.

Now breathing again, Charlie wanted to look around, so he opened only one eye in order to minimize the fright factor. Seeing nothing in the vicinity, Charlie moved to check on his friend down at the bottom of the ditch. "Gene, are you okay?" he asked, looking 15 or 20 feet downward.

Gene was lying still, flat on his back at the bottom of the dirt hill. He said nothing for nearly half a minute.

Eventually he asked in a very weak voice, "Are we still alive?" Clearly he was totally traumatized.

"Yes, we were lucky to get through that little scrape," said Charlie to Gene far below him.

"*Little scrape?!*" Gene apparently had regained his voice, and sat up somewhat in order to raise an objection. "That's the most horrible thing I've ever seen, and ten times worse than anything I've ever imagined," he said in forceful disagreement with Charlie.

Charlie and Betty (still on leash) slid down the dirt hill, trying to keep their feet, toward the virtually insensate man at the ditch bottom, to offer support. As they got there, Betty licked Gene's face as if to revivify him.

"Well, that was a classic bigfoot bluff charge, my friend," explained Charlie to Gene, who was now pulling himself together and starting to scale the dirt hill. "The big primates do that sometimes to…discourage…creatures they're not terribly fond of at that moment."

"*Not terribly fond of?!*" cried Gene as he turned to look at Charlie, with the same aghast tone as his prior question. "I have never been so close to certain death in all my years, and I don't ever want to experience that again. Can we leave now?"

"Well, before we go let's see if we can do a quick height estimate on this individual," said Charlie as he and his dog made their way slowly back up the dirt precipice. Reaching the top, Charlie walked to the spot where the creature left the area.

Gene wasn't pleased. With Charlie and Betty leading the way, Gene very slowly walked over to the spot with extreme hesitation, looking around in all directions to ensure that the monster had left the area.

Arriving at the spot, Charlie took out his measuring tape yet again. He aimed the partially unspooled tape up to a mid-sized branch nine or ten feet up.

He said to the Gene, "I think the top of his head was roughly even with this branch, wouldn't you agree?"

Gene seemed in no hurry to reply to any further stimuli. He shook his head, squinted his eyes briefly and eventually replied, "Aw heck, maybe that's about right." He quickly added, "But who cares?! We barely survived this dang monster and now it's time to skedaddle."

Charlie extended the tape measure out and ran it up the tree. "Just under nine feet up, I'd say," he said suddenly, having gotten as close as he could to estimating the creature's height. He had taken such measurements and issued such estimates many times before in his avocational investigating career, although with no physical evidence remaining, the measurements could not be considered precise in any way.

"Geez, nine feet tall," replied Gene with pained comprehension. "I'm glad as hell he took off."

Charlie rapidly assessed the area a bit more, took a few more photos of the creature's exit point tree, the cable spool and some footprints, and then the group headed back the way they came on the trail. Wholly tired of forest exploits for the day, Gene led the way with alacrity.

As they walked, Charlie said to Gene, "I'd certainly like to make a track cast of that clear footprint I measured and photographed up here a bit. Myrtle's currently got possession of my casting materials."

"Uh, who's Myrtle?" asked Gene with some fatigued befuddlement.

"Oh, I forgot to tell you," said Charlie. "Motor Myrtle's the name of our RV. I see her as a full partner in this type of peripatetic enterprise, so she certainly deserves a name."

Once again, Gene didn't really have a reasoned response to Charlie's comment. "Oh, whatever," was all he said, walking sullenly with head down.

"But you know, man," he suddenly interspersed, "you're on your own with casting that thing. I don't care about it. I want to go home, and I want to go home now." There was no mistaking Gene's level of upset.

For Gene's sake, picking up the pace now as they proceeded back toward the house and once again spotting the clear footprint, Charlie left a large rock next to it for ease of subsequent location.

Soon the trio got back to the house and the RV, where Charlie grabbed his plaster of paris, water and other needed materials. Charlie told Gene they'd be back in an hour or less. The favorable footprint wasn't too far afield, so Charlie and Betty would make the short trip themselves.

Slamming the back door, Gene went noisily into the house, likely to grab and hold onto a stair railing or sink edge for upright stability, given his stunned amazement at what the group had just witnessed (and very nearly been attacked by) in the woods.

Arriving back at the track, Charlie started mixing the plaster in a bucket in proportions of roughly one part water to two parts plaster. After mixing it up, he dumped the thickening white goop into the large footprint and smoothed it out somewhat with a small trowel so that the eventual back of the cast would be relatively flat.

Charlie and Betty would need to wait in place until the track cast fully dried and solidified. Charlie thought about letting Betty off of her leash to allow her to explore a little bit, but remembering the nine-foot-tall furniture felon in the vicinity, Charlie decided to play it safe with his dog. He talked to her about the prospect of getting home soon and seeing mommy (i.e., Francesca) again soon.

After a wait of about 45 minutes, Charlie began scraping away dirt around the edges of the white cast. Carefully touching the solid plaster form from all directions, Charlie decided that it was dry enough to extract from the ground. He then very carefully and gently dug the cast out and scraped off small clumps of dirt from where they were sticking to the track. As in North Carolina previously, Charlie's cast-making efforts resulted in a fairly clean track cast—always a highly welcome accomplishment.

Charlie wrapped up the cast in some paper towels, packed up his gear and accompanied Betty back down the trail toward Gene's house carrying his new trackway treasure.

Getting back to Gene's property, Charlie headed straight to Motor Myrtle in the driveway to stow his new block of evidence and his casting supplies. He brought Betty inside the rig to give her an opportunity to catch up on some rest, given yet another fearful, draining adventure in the far-off woods this day.

Gene stepped off his porch and walked slowly up to the rig, looking quite discontented with hands in back pockets and a slightly scowling face. Charlie saw Gene approaching, and stepped out to talk with him.

"Charlie, I cannot *believe* that thing we saw out there. It never occurred to me that bigfoot might be among all the animals we see around here. I guess I've had my mind pretty much pried open and rewired, and I'm not too happy about it."

"Yes, my newly distressed Missourian friend, bigfoot will do that to you," replied Charlie with gentle understanding. "For most witnesses, their first (and sometimes only) encounter with this creature is a life-changing experience at the very least. All the truths they thought they knew about the natural world get pitched forcibly into the ditch (so to speak), and they struggle with the fact that they won't ever see the world the same way again. And *some* of us (ahem!) go way down the bunny hole and keep pursuing these creatures despite plentiful indications that the quest is Quixote-like at best, and dang ludicrous at worst."

Gene appreciated Charlie's off-kilter worldview description. "Well, you got us up close and personal with a real-life monster today, and pulled in a bunch of evidence, I imagine. I'm sorry this quest ends up being so looney to you, but you're good at what you do—I can tell," said Gene, softening somewhat. "Just don't include me again, please."

"My skills at being looney are surpassed only by my insatiable appetite for all things of high caloric content," said Charlie, patting his own slightly swollen tummy as he spoke.

"And speaking of that," began Gene, taking a new tack, "would you join Rebecca and me for some dinner tonight? I promise we won't have rabbits or bigfoots or loonies or anything like that on the menu...maybe just something boring and safe like pizza."

"I'd be delighted, regardless, kind sir," replied Charlie gracefully with a courtly nod of his head.

"And also," said Gene, "where are you planning to stay tonight? It's getting kind of late and you're sort of way out here."

"Uh, given our slightly...ambitious itinerary today," said Charlie, "I'll admit that I haven't given the lodging issue any thought at all." He scratched his bearded chin and scrunched up his lips in sudden contemplation.

"Well, you're welcome to stay overnight with your rig here in the driveway if you'd like," said Gene, "or you could even come inside for the night, and—heaven forbid—actually sleep indoors. I think tonight I'll be sleeping in our wall safe."

Charlie giggled at Gene's slightly bumpy invitation. "I believe Betty and I would be very comfortable out here within the Myrtle mobile. If I could just run a three-prong cable up to your house to borrow a bit of power for generating heat and the like, that would be absolutely ideal."

"Oh certainly, Charlie, you guys can hook up for all you're worth," said Gene, suggesting that he might have had some knowledge of the logistics of RV life.

With that, Charlie opened one of the side storage panels on Myrtle and extracted a power cord and an adapter so that his 50-amp power could translate to a 15-amp, 120-volt home plug-in. That way he'd get at least some power to the RV overnight. Gene ran the long cord into the garage for Charlie and plugged it into the closest outlet.

Charlie and Betty joined Gene and Rebecca for dinner. Gene's wife had, indeed, ordered a couple of pizzas from a local pizzeria while Charlie was out in the field forming his track cast.

At table, over slices of pepperoni, ham and extra cheese, Charlie asked, "Are you doing better now, Gene?"

Gene covered his eyes with a hand, then replied in a highly downcast fashion, "God, I don't know."

"You know," said Rebecca to Charlie, "I've never seen my husband like this."

Gene jumped right back in, saying, "You're just lucky that you're seeing your husband *at all*, I'd say."

"It was a pretty close call out there, Rebecca," Charlie explained. "We happened upon an oversized individual who didn't like other cooks entering his kitchen."

At this point Charlie was surprised to see two beagles enter the dining room—his Betty girl and another, much larger tricolor canine.

"Ah, this is Chaco," said Rebecca. "He's our monster beagle; he might be mixed with a Basset or something. We're not sure."

Chaco walked slowly into the adjacent living room, jumped up on a leather loveseat, laid down and promptly fell asleep. Betty climbed right up next to him and snuggled in, with her head at his sizeable caboose.

"Wow, these two could be good buds," said Rebecca pleasingly as she looked on.

"I don't think Chaco would like bigfoot any more than Betty did today," said Gene, slightly gruffly.

"Right, well, dogs and sasquatches are rather notorious adversaries, or at least not the closest of friends," said Charlie.

The group was quiet for several minutes, enjoying the cheesy, crusty delight of hot pizza.

Before long, however, Charlie initiated one of his philosophical excursions as the group was still pondering what had happened.

"You know, one must wonder at the motivation of such a creature to make off with a hundred-and-something-pound spool and lug it a mile into the forest," said Charlie to the others.

Rebecca piped up, saying, "It doesn't make any sense to me, but it's astounding."

"Astounding might be considered an understatement," said Charlie in reaction.

Continuing his fanciful theorization, Charlie said, "One could posit that the sasquatch was attempting to arrange a romantic dinner with a mate, and borrowed the spool as an item of epicurean accoutrement."

The table was again quiet as Gene and Rebecca struggled to grasp what Charlie was saying. He looked at them and realized this. Betty and Chaco had both fallen asleep in the next room.

"In other words, maybe the big guy was going to give his girl a gourmet surprise, but she stood him up at the ravine!" clarified Charlie jovially and with a smile.

He continued. "And you know, males of many species have been known to tear down the drapes when romantic disappointments occur. Our nine-footer may have had the best of intentions but had his hairy hopes dashed upon being spurned by a discourteous damsel. Ha!"

Wide-eyed, both Rebecca and Gene looked questioningly at each other, then at Charlie, in an attempt to track with his far-flung theory.

"I have no idea what that crazy creature was up to, but I've never seen anything move so fast, and I'm never going to that area of the forest again," said Gene resolutely. "And another thing: I sure as shootin' hope that thing doesn't return here to the house."

"Well, as painful as it was today, Gene," Charlie said, "once you recover you'll be able to tell a whopper of a fun story for the rest of your life."

Gene just stared at Charlie blankly for several seconds, then closed his eyes and shook his head. "Fun, huh? I could do without such a damn 'fun story.'" Rebecca wasn't sure whether Gene was going to hurl a slice of pizza at Charlie or not.

"Well," began Charlie breezily—clearly recognizing the need to rapidly change the subject—"perhaps we should talk about how good this pizza is. Thank you so much, Rebecca, for arranging this feast."

The dinner continued apace, albeit rather quietly, after which Charlie and Betty headed out to the sleeping comforts of Motor Myrtle. The big beagle boy Chaco looked like he would probably have wanted Betty to stay around, but the smaller beagle seemed more than willing to get back into the vehicle for a good night's sleep in preparation for tomorrow's departure.

Before turning in for the night, Charlie checked his messages. He had heard from an old bigfooting friend, Emmi Flowers, who lived in Fruitland, New Mexico—in the far northwestern corner of the state. Charlie knew Emmi from past bigfoot conferences and expeditions.

Emmi's message said that someone known to her family had a terrifying experience recently with one of the fabled forest giants, and Charlie was welcome to come take an investigative look if he wanted to. Replying by text, Charlie enthusiastically accepted the invitation. Motor Myrtle would head out early the next morning for New Mexico—Charlie and Betty's home state.

13

FEAR IN THE FOUR CORNERS

Prior to leaving Prairie Home early the next morning, Charlie steered Motor Myrtle to a small but reputable diner he'd heard about. There he ordered and enjoyed a pancake and syrup breakfast with sausage and several cups of coffee. Returning to Motor Myrtle afterward, Charlie watched Betty happily scarf down the sausage scraps he'd brought her.

Getting out onto I-70 and heading west on this sunny November day, the travel group stayed on the big highway for some time. They crossed out of Missouri and began the long westward trek across Kansas. Just short of midway through the state, Charlie pulled Motor Myrtle over for a break in Salina. He hit up a Little Italy-style restaurant for some pizza slices featuring smoked salmon. Betty was positively thrilled at this luxurious, unusually fishy takeout-box delicacy.

Later, Charlie and the group exited I-70 in Oakley, Kansas and stopped overnight at High Plains Camping. The facility had a fenced-in dog run where, just before dark, Betty got to cavort with a salt-and-pepper Miniature Schnauzer, a black Scottie dog and a lovable black Labrador Retriever. Afterward, Charlie visited a rare on-site pub and got to cavort with some cold brews.

The next morning, the group continued onward along I-70, crossing the Colorado state line and driving west through the beautiful Rocky Mountain state. Having picked up CO-71 and traveled directly south for some time, they stopped in the town of Rocky Ford for some diner food, then continued southwest into New Mexico. They eventually took US-64 and rode that west all the way to the town of Fruitland in the far northwest corner of the state.

The New Mexico portion of the Four Corners region (i.e., the convergence of Arizona, Colorado, New Mexico and Utah) was well known for bigfoot sightings, encounters, and other slightly odd events; legends of unexplained creatures went back many years in this area. Charlie was excited to be getting to this spot, just across the San Juan River from the Navajo Nation, not only because he was back in his home state but because he had wanted to investigate sasquatch activity in this region for some time—yet never had until now.

Very late in the day, Motor Myrtle pulled into the town of Fruitland, where his SSDD colleague, Emmi Flowers, resided. A family she knew there had recently reported a very unsettling encounter with a renowned occasional visitor to the area—a hungry sasquatch, apparently.

Typical of high-desert topography, the terrain in this corner of New Mexico was mostly open land, with stands of low trees (e.g., juniper and piñon) interspersed among residential neighborhoods, ancient volcanic rock escarpments serving as natural enclosures, and salt cedar trees and larger cottonwood trees lining the rocky shores of the bosque (a term meaning "trees by the river")—in this case the San Juan River.

Charlie navigated Motor Myrtle to the home address he had on file for Emmi and stopped there just off Road 6700, which runs somewhat parallel to US-64. Many but not all of the residences in this area were single- and double-wide mobile homes. The RV rolled to a stop in Emmi's gravel driveway on a cool, sunny afternoon.

As Charlie was gathering some gear and getting ready to visit with Emmi, she walked out of the house and came up to Myrtle to welcome the crew. She was a petite, effervescent, late 30-something woman of Native American descent with luxurious, long black hair. She was wearing a Denver Broncos jersey and blue jeans.

Charlie opened a side door of the RV and Emmi said cheerfully, "Hi there, Charlie. Welcome...*back*...to New Mexico!"

This of course put a smile on Charlie's face as he reveled in the kindness of a "neighbor" who knew of his travel circuit.

"It's wonderful to see you again, Emmi!" he said jovially. He stepped down out of the rig and gave Emmi a hearty hug.

"And who might this be?" asked Emmi as Betty jumped down from the bottom step of the RV.

"Why, this is my crew supervisor, Betty," said Charlie with typical flair.

"Hi there, girl!" said Emmi warmly to Betty, who ran right up to the now-kneeling Emmi and received a profusion of ear and back scratches. Emmi got some licks on the cheek. Charlie could quickly tell that Emmi was an animal lover.

"Does she help you with investigations?" Emmi asked.

"Oh, she's a help all right. Just on this trip alone she's angered a veritable handful of sasquatches who have shown their canine contempt in no uncertain terms."

"Really?!" asked Emmi breathlessly. "You'll have to tell me about those."

"And certainly I will," replied Charlie. "Emmi, it's rather late in the day now, so would it be okay with you if I docked Motor Myrtle in your driveway here overnight?"

Stopped in her mental tracks, Emmi had no idea what Charlie was talking about. "Who is Motor Myrtle?" she asked.

"Oh, forgive me, Emmi," Charlie said. "That's our nickname for this rolling sardine can—the esteemed RV of choice for unmoored sasquatch antagonists everywhere."

Emmi laughed, though she didn't quite grasp every nuance of Charlie's oddball sentence.

"And would you mind if I hooked up my RV electric to your house?" he then asked.

"Oh sure, that's fine. Just give me your power cord when you're ready, and I'll get it plugged in."

As he did in Missouri previously, Charlie extracted his cord and adapter so that he could tap into residential 120-volt power. He carried the cable end to Emmi, and she ran it up to her front porch for the plug-in. Charlie would thus be able to grab some heat in the rig tonight if things got too cold for comfort.

"So, have you had much activity in the area recently?" Charlie asked Emmi as they finished with the power practicalities. By "activity," Emmi knew exactly what Charlie was talking about.

"Yes, we don't seem to go very long before we have another sighting," she replied. "Not too far back we had a big brown- or red-haired thing spotted walking along the river over here," said Emmi, gesturing in the direction of the area's large waterway, the San Juan. "The sheriff even saw it at one point. The creature apparently stunk to high heaven, and it made a bunch of loud howls at night. Lots of us heard that."

"Interesting," said Charlie, thoughtfully, as he scratched his chin in creature contemplation.

"We also had a neighbor who heard someone messing around in his shed late at night about three months ago," said Emmi. "He went out there with a flashlight and this huge, hairy thing more than seven feet tall—he said—was rummaging around in the shed. It apparently had to duck down to come back outside, then it turned and loped away into the brush. The homeowner was pretty darn scared."

"Goodness me," exclaimed Charlie. "And this was close by, you say?"

"Yep, just a few blocks away from here."

"This almost sounds like a hotspot to me," remarked Charlie with a tone of wonderment.

"Well, I'm guessing that these creatures routinely move up and down the river," explained Emmi, "finding food however they can.

Whereas there are certainly food sources in and around the river—plus the adjacent fields where we grow corn and melons and things—I think these creatures get curious sometimes and they come up into the residential areas to see what's up." She emitted a slight giggle after sharing her theory of sasquatch sightseeing.

"I wouldn't doubt it a bit," replied Charlie summarily.

By this time, the sun had gone down and it was almost time to turn in for the night.

"Emmi, I think Betty and I will close up shop and call it a night out here," he said. "We put a lot miles on today."

"Okay, well, just let me know if you need anything," she said politely.

"See you in the early a.m., okay?" he asked.

"Yes, maybe eight or nine a.m.—not *too* early," Emmi said with a friendly sleep-in oriented smile. "I got some fresh bagels today that we can share tomorrow morning."

"That sounds lovely in every way," said Charlie in his extra-gracious manner.

Returning to Motor Myrtle, Charlie heated up a frozen pot pie. It was a road-practical though not glamorous repast. After also feeding Betty, Charlie hooked her up and took her for a leisurely walk around the mostly dark neighborhood. As the sounds of traffic started to diminish in the deepening darkness and the late hour, Charlie could more clearly hear the soothing sound of moving water in the nearby river. He also enjoyed the fragrance of New Mexico nature at night, which he hadn't experienced in months.

Charlie and Betty strolled back to Motor Myrtle and turned in for the night.

After a restful night of RV sleep in Emmi's driveway, Charlie got Betty out for an early morning stroll around the neighborhood—this time with visible items of terrain, habitation and transportation. (In other words, they could see where the heck they were going this time, and wouldn't walk into as many parked cars.)

Waiting for Charlie and Betty on her front porch, Emmi and her brown Miniature Pinscher, Brutus, greeted them as they returned from their walk. She invited them inside for breakfast. Neither guest protested in the least. Excited Betty and Brutus performed all of the obligatory sniff ceremonials as they entered the house.

At a sunny breakfast nook table, Emmi had the bagels and dairy toppings spread out, along with juice, milk and coffee.

"Good gracious, what a welcome display this is!" exclaimed Charlie at the sight.

"I hope you enjoy it, Charlie," replied Emmi. "Oh, and you can let Betty have the run of the place. She'll be fine." Charlie quickly unclipped Betty from her leash and the dog ran off to explore the house and tumble with the similarly sized Brutus.

"Now, you be good, young lady!" admonished Charlie firmly to his canine companion.

As Emmi and Charlie ate, they discussed the subjects of their meeting set for later this morning. They would apparently be meeting with some close-by neighbors, the Martinez family, whose children recently had a too-close-for-comfort encounter with a hungry "hairy man." Still over breakfast, Emmi verbally sketched the rough outline of the story for Charlie, but didn't include excess detail so that he could gather the information he found most relevant and valuable.

Emmi and Charlie mutually decided to leave the dogs to their own devices in the home while the humans visited elsewhere.

"Please don't eat the furniture, my dear," said Charlie dramatically to Betty as the investigative duo closed up and headed out to Emmi's car.

They drove not even a minute and a half, with only one or two vehicle turns, to the spot where the monster encounter apparently took place, a residence on Road 6740, which ended in a cul-de-sac at the very edge of the bosque. Charlie duly noted how close this residence was to the river.

Knocking on the front door of the white one-story residence, Emmi was pleased when Jackie Martinez came to the door with her husband Luis following closely behind. The hosts welcomed the two visitors. Jackie hugged Emmi, while Charlie and Luis shook hands. Charlie was lugging his backpack.

"So, I understand you had an interesting visitor here," said Emmi to the hosts, whose numbers increased when a boy and girl of pre-teen age entered the living room and sat down.

"Yes, Angel and Antonio here had quite the experience," said Jackie, pointing to the girl and boy in respective order.

"Hello there, young friends, I'm Charlie Marlowe" said the sasquatch investigator to his two new young charges, shaking hands with them in turn.

As the introductions and other preliminaries proceeded, Charlie extracted his laptop and prepared for what he hoped would be a healthy stretch of notetaking.

Angel Martinez, a slight, cute girl with olive skin and pretty dark brown hair—probably about ten years of age in Charlie's estimation—began recounting the tale as Charlie started typing.

"Well, my friend Melissa and I were sitting out on the front porch," said Angel. "It was like late morning or something. We were on our phones or whatever. Right around the same time, we both saw this huge, dark, man-looking thing standing at the edge of our property. It may have come around from the back yard, which goes right out to the bosque. I don't know. But it was only about 80 or 100 feet away, just standing there looking at us. We got a good look at it, and we both got *real* scared."

"Can you tell me what the creature looked like, Angel?" asked Charlie in a polite manner, with fingers rapidly tapping laptop keys, as usual.

"Yeah, I guess so. It was very dark brown or maybe black, and it had four- or five-inch-long hair of that color all over its body," said Angel. "It was really hairy. It didn't have any clothes, so I knew it wasn't a man. That was *weird*. As it stood there in front of the bushes, I could see that its hands hung way down to around its knees. That was also pretty weird, and it made me sure this wasn't a regular person. To Melissa and me, the creature looked like something maybe between a tall gorilla and a human being, but it was *really* tall—maybe seven or eight feet—and real strong, with big muscles. Its face looked...kind of human," Angel concluded.

Angel reported that she had quickly run inside with Melissa (and locked the front door) to report the encounter to whomever was home at that time. Her brother, twelve-year-old Antonio, took note of her alarm and walked around the perimeter of the house to check for intruders, but he didn't see anything unusual.

At this point in the present, amidst the full family and the visiting investigators, Antonio took up the narrative. He was a fairly tall, thin boy with close-cropped dark hair, wearing a Metallica t-shirt.

"After that, I went back to my room where my friend Mikey and I had been playing video games. Man, he *sucks* at 'Call of Duty: Black Ops.' I was basically destroying him." (Antonio chuckled to himself with overt self-satisfaction.)

"Anyway, about ten minutes later, we heard all these crashing noises coming from the living room or somewhere at the front of the house. It sounded like someone was throwing crap around the place. That was way weird," offered Antonio.

Antonio's father shrugged up one shoulder, perhaps lightly bristling at the slight coarseness of his son's descriptions.

However, at this point in the encounter event, all four of the kids apparently ran almost simultaneously out of the bedrooms to the living room to see what the clatter and commotion was all about.

"When we got out to the living room," said Angel, picking up the retelling, "we see this big, giant, hairy hand reaching through the front window. I guess it had pulled off the screen, maybe. On the end table under the window right here, there was a bowl with wrapped candy in it. The creature was grabbing that bowl, trying to run off with the treats, I guess. It had knocked over a lamp and a stack of books and some other stuff."

"Yeah, but then these girls started screaming like *crazy*," interjected Antonio. "I think that thing got scared to death by all that girl noise, so he dropped the bowl, pulled his arm back out and walked off...without any candy." Antonio again chuckled to himself.

However, the disconcerting story did not symmetrically end there.

Antonio resumed the narrative. "After I was pretty sure the thing was gone, I walked out around the house some more. Again, I didn't see anyone—and that was pretty strange," he said.

"Yes, and we were at Walmart finishing our shopping," reported Jackie abruptly, as if to provide a rationale for the parents' absence.

"So I walked a little further out front toward the main road," resumed Antonio, "when I see this big thing again, way across the street—maybe a football field's length away from me. It wasn't real close, but I didn't like what I was seeing. And it was looking back at me. I ran back to the house pretty fast."

At this juncture of the encounter, Antonio experienced a highly tangible example of the creature's capacities.

"I got to the front door—*right outside here* (Antonio pointed)—and when I turned around right before coming inside, that thing was standing about 15 feet behind me, just staring at me with its muscles all clenched, right out here on the walkway. *It had chased me all the way back to the house*, and *crazy fast!*" concluded Antonio, with obvious astonishment.

As the boy reported this very close scrape with a huge, apparently speedy monster, he put his head down in his hands and shook it from side to side somewhat.

Looking up again and resuming his description in a pained tone, he said, "I closed that door so fast and locked it, then I ran around the house and made sure all the other doors—and windows too—were locked. Geez, that thing was unbelievable," he concluded.

The living room was entirely quiet after Antonio and Angel finished their harrowing account of a huge, intrusive monster. Charlie was more than willing to let the dust settle after this unnerving retelling.

"We were very proud of Antonio for doing what he had to do to protect the household," said his dad Luis.

Charlie let this affirming comment hang for several seconds as he observed the two young people—both still clearly traumatized by what they had seen in and around their home. Angel was tapping her foot quickly and staring off into space, while Antonio had put his head down in his hands again.

"Well, Angel," Charlie asked, trying to get back on a constructive track, "Did you get a good *second* look at the creature, when it extended its arm through the window?"

Angel gradually replied, "Um, I saw the face pretty well but I didn't see much of the rest of the body. That big, hairy arm coming through the window was *way* scary, so I didn't see it standing up this time or anything," she added.

At this point, Antonio piped up and added, "That monster was so much bigger than a man that I couldn't believe it. Plus it smelled awful, like dead fish and rotten eggs or something super gross."

"Yup, it was nasty," added Angel.

Charlie took time to document the details that the young people provided.

Then Angel's mother added, "Even though their father and I didn't see the creature, the disgusting smell lingered in here for a long time. Not even a bunch of clouds of air freshener spray helped very much."

The father in turn said, "And now we've told the kids to be very careful and stay right by the house, night and day. We have no idea if that big thing is coming back, but I guess it might."

The father reported that other neighbors had seen the creature at the edges of fields and down by the river recently, and they'd heard strange calls or cries late at night.

"Well, that is all *most* remarkable," commented Charlie.

Emmi added, "These folks have been through it, all right. You kids were very brave."

Angel smiled just a little at her big brother and then her parents, tapping her feet quickly in response to the compliment.

Charlie finished typing up the family's account to this point, then asked if he could inspect the window where the creature had reached inside.

Luis said, "Yes, of course, whatever you need."

"Kids, can you tell me exactly where the creature's arm was when you saw it come in the window, and also tell me how far inside it reached?" asked Charlie.

Angel walked a few steps over to the front window and pointed to the spot where the huge arm had apparently come through.

"It came right through here," she said as she was pointing, then added, "and the candy bowl was right here on the table," indicating roughly the center of the small table beneath the front window.

"I found the destroyed screen later out on the porch," said Luis.

"Really? Can we see it if it's still around?" inquired Emmi quickly.

"Sure, I think it's still out there."

He, Charlie and Emmi walked out the front door to locate the crumpled screen. By now the screen was all the way down at the far end of the porch—bent and mangled into a pure piece of pointy metal garbage. Luis picked up the wrecked screen and presented it to Emmi and Charlie.

"Wow, the big fellow sure finished off this screen, didn't he?" said Charlie, without expecting a reply. He turned the twisted metal and screen over in his hands a few times and observed it very closely to see if there was any hair or blood visible anywhere. There wasn't.

"I know bigfoots like to forage all over for food, but candy in wrappers...and candy that's *inside* the house?! Man, oh man, that's a new one on me," commented Emmi as the group continued to communally ponder the encounter that happened here.

Emmi and Charlie, followed by Luis, headed back inside and made certain to earnestly thank each Martinez child for their very helpful reporting of what had happened to them. Charlie shook hands vigorously with both Angel and Antonio, showering them with effusive praise. The investigators also sincerely thanked Jackie and Luis for their time, and for giving the investigators unfettered access to their slightly traumatized children.

As they were saying their goodbyes to the family at the front door, Emmi and Charlie were both surprised by Jackie's revisiting of a theme she had touched upon previously.

With her head tilted downward a bit, she said rather sheepishly, "You know, I hope you don't think we were irresponsible in leaving the kids home alone when something like this happened..."

Jackie did not look at all comfortable as she obliquely sought a degree of parental validation, and perhaps a diminution of parental guilt.

"Oh of *course* not, Jackie," replied Charlie rapidly, with a wide, helpful smile. "You know, if you were to sit around in life waiting for one of these monstrous, hairy bipeds to show up on the front porch, you'd likely be waiting between 80 and 740 years. Imagine the tax implications of such a stretch."

All of the adults giggled at Charlie's admittedly successful effort to put things into better perspective and lighten things up for the Martinez family. Secretly, both he and Emmi wondered if the huge interloper might return to this spot sometime. However, that would result in an investigation for another day—perhaps 80 or 740 years away.

The investigators finally took their leave and made the shockingly short drive back to Emmi's house.

Unloading their respective gear back at Emmi's place, Charlie and Emmi each attended to activities of interest. After checking on Betty (no household furniture was destroyed), Charlie set up his laptop on the shaded, screened-in back porch and touched up his witness notes, while Emmi made her way to the kitchen, returning to the porch with some iced tea in a pitcher. Over the cold beverages, the two veteran bigfooters traded monster stories.

Emmi asked Charlie about his adventures on this current trip, and as usual, Charlie spun out some highlights of accounts that his listener might find interesting. These included recent "greatest hits" like the huge snake-slinging monster of Texas, the stump-chucking sasquatch of Louisiana, the preteen porch monster in Florida, the snow-stepping giant of Michigan and the monstrous cable table crook of Prairie Home, Missouri.

"Wow, you sure have seen the sasquatch sights, Charlie," exclaimed Emmi. "Maybe I'll come along with you and Betty next time..."

"That would be an adventure indeed," responded Charlie. "We've covered lots of ground on this trip but by no means have we hit all the bigfoot hotspots that this huge country has to offer."

While Emmi was quite impressed by Charlie's brief accounts, she added several of her own—most reported by residents of the immediate area. They included a local man's sighting of a large, bipedal night monster in a sheep camp in the nearby mountains, a driver's account of seeing a broad, more than seven-foot-tall creature charging up a hill next to a highway, and reports of huge, cave-dwelling, manlike creatures making their way down into the river valley to forage for unsupervised crops during harvest season.

Charlie listened intently to Emmi and was fascinated by the richness of the stories she shared. At one point he remarked that perhaps he shouldn't be traveling so far afield when there are so many bigfoot encounters occurring in certain corners of his home state of New Mexico.

After a while, Emmi invited Charlie and Betty inside for some dinner. She made chicken enchiladas with spicy green chilé sauce, with smoky pinto beans and cheese on the side. They continued to enjoy mutual sasquatch "shop talk." Meanwhile, Betty and Brutus lay near each other on the kitchen floor, watching for available leavings. There weren't many that were suitable for dogs after the somewhat fiery New Mexican meal. Charlie thanked Emmi for her generous hospitality.

After dinner, all four creatures headed to the back yard for some outdoor playtime as the sun descended. The dogs had a great time charging around the yard, taking in the scents and wrestling occasionally. Although the back yard was fenced in, Charlie watched Betty closely due to the recent presence of a large, agile, intelligent monster in the area.

As it got dark, Charlie reminded Emmi that he and Betty would be leaving for home early the next morning.

"Oh, right, I'm sorry you can't stay longer, Charlie, but I know you're looking forward to a home-cooked meal," said Emmi, referencing Charlie's certain spousal appreciation.

"Actually, at this moment I'm looking backward at a lovely enchilada meal; that was completely scrumptious!" said Charlie with a giggle. Emmi appreciated the compliment.

The bigfooters gave each other a goodbye hug, and Charlie and Betty headed to the rig for the night. Charlie again thanked Emmi emphatically for the thoughtful kindness she had extended toward the somewhat road-weary duo.

After dark, Charlie called Francesca on the cell to tell her that he was now in-state and was planning to be home sometime the next day. They talked both about current goings on at the Marlowe residence and the welfare of the two road warriors.

Early on during their conversation, Francesca said to Charlie, "I can't *believe* the proverbial wayfaring stranger is approaching the home front at last. Unfortunately, though, I don't think there's room for you to park the RV here; I've taken a shopworn circus under my wing, and the clown cars and elephants tend to take up most of the driveway."

Charlie laughed at his spouse's consistently crafty comedy. "Very funny, my dear," he replied. "Maybe I can solicit the help of some clowns in fixing those backyard drip system problems you mentioned."

"Oh, that project was already full of clown capers the last time you attended to it," Francesca editorialized.

Charlie could only shake his head and smile at his wife's clever zingers.

Soon the couple said goodnight, and Charlie and Betty got comfortable on one of the rig's beds. They anticipated nothing but a quiet, high-desert doze.

It was the middle of the night when Charlie suddenly awoke to the unusual sensation of a driverless Motor Myrtle in motion. Jolted from a sound sleep, Charlie didn't know whether an earthquake had struck or a large alien craft had crashed right next to or into the rig.

However, the movement of the RV soon became quite terrestrially violent. Charlie began to wonder (somewhat irrationally) if the back passenger portion of the vehicle would be pulled off of the underlying truck bed—the shaking was so intense. It felt like the vehicle was being pushed so hard that it was teetering up onto two wheels. Meanwhile Betty had awoken and was barking at whatever malevolent force was nearly toppling the truck. She was trying to stand up and look out the window, but the tremors were too strong. Metal items throughout the vehicle clanged loudly, and camping supplies inside jostled about and toppled noisily off of shelves.

"Hold on, girl!" yelled Charlie to his temporarily discombobulated dog as he made his way forward to the cab. Struggling to keep his feet amidst the upheaval, Charlie got to the driver's seat and flicked on the headlights, simultaneously depressing the horn button at the center of the steering console.

Fortunately, this action stopped whatever was shaking the vehicle. Charlie looked out each window of the RV, trying to spot the source of the shaking. He didn't see anything. He walked back to the bunk area to check on Betty. He sat down on the bed next to her and offered some petting comfort. At this point, the dog was not the only creature requiring comfort.

"I don't know what in tarnation that was, girl, but it was pretty powerful," he said as he smoothed the ruffled, agitated hair along the little dog's back.

Suddenly a sound unlike any other came from just behind the RV, perhaps five feet away from the man and his dog.

It was a vicious, powerful scream that shot up from a deep growl to a midrange screech—in just seconds—that nearly made the man and dog simultaneously pass out in fear. The creature's vocalization had all the low-frequency power of the largest animals on the planet...and then some.

Charlie had heard lots of roars and hoots and whoops over the years, but the close proximity of this monstrous bigfoot blast was utterly jarring and totally terrifying. Betty went flat on the bed with her head plastered down into the covers.

Charlie moved to look out the back window, which, to his amazement, was mostly filled with the sight of a huge, conical head, a dark face with a large nose, and two fully frightening, slightly glowing eyes staring intently at him.

"Geez, I think the neighborhood monster found us," whispered Charlie to the unspecified atmosphere.

He then heard a couple of quick advancing footsteps followed by a titanic smash, as if something had run up and slammed the back of the vehicle with a telephone pole or cinder block. The crash was accompanied by a sharp, angry-seeming breath expulsion from a large creature. The creature's impact again made the entire vehicle shimmy in response, moving back and forth. Charlie nearly fell from his seated position.

"Holy hedge whackers!!!" he shouted to his again-flattened dog. "This thing is less than pleased, I'd say."

Charlie then heard the sound of slower, steadier, heavy footfalls receding into the distance. He hoped that the clearly agitated sasquatch had chosen another destination.

Sitting totally still for about five minutes, Charlie didn't hear another sound. By now he was fairly sure that the creature had left the immediate area.

"Well, I guess we're going to live...this time...Miss Betty," said Charlie to his woebegone beagle pal as he gently scratched her ears.

With the welcome silence and stillness stretching toward 15 minutes, Charlie moved to a nearby shelf to grab and down a near-empty bottle of red wine as a nerve-calming measure. He quickly swigged what was left of the vinegary liquid.

"Maybe we should take up Icelandic music appreciation, girl," he said to the dog as he looked out the windows one last time for the night...in complete bewilderment over what had just occurred. He decided there would be no value in looking around outside for evidence of tattered vehicle components or anything else. He truly hoped that Motor Myrtle would be able to recover and complete the journey tomorrow.

It took the dog and her human more than a half hour to even begin to settle down from the night-shattering, monster-driven, quaky encounter they'd had. Sleep did *not* come easily.

At first light, Charlie looked around the RV to assess the state of affairs. While he was one hundred percent certain that a large creature had terrorized the vehicle and its occupants last night, he could see no apparent footprints in the dry gravel driveway.

Inspecting the back of the vehicle, however, Charlie observed a different story. Right below the rear window was a matching set of dents in the metal, approximately the size of softballs. The creature's twin thumps had left deep dimples in the metal. Charlie was fully amazed at the superhuman power that must have been required to impress the metal in such a way. That, plus the ferocious shaking of the large vehicle, was an impressive display of brute animal force. Someone (or more likely some *thing*) clearly took umbrage at the presence of an unfamiliar vehicle at this location. Charlie secretly wished that the monster had spotted the New Mexico license plate on the big rig—and recognized a neighbor.

Regardless, soon Charlie knocked on Emmi's door to inform her about what had happened overnight. She appeared at the door in a robe and slippers. Whereas Charlie's original plan was to leave in the early a.m. with no further contact, he decided he should report his experience to Emmi; she would likely find his account—occurring right in her driveway—quite compelling and significant.

"I heard the truck horn and the scream last night," she said. "I thought about coming outside, but that thing sounded way upset and was bashing things," she said. "Looks like you were hanging with the locals last night."

"Well, I appreciate local color as much as the next guy, but that thing nearly tipped Motor Myrtle over and left us in the dust," said Charlie, without much exaggeration.

He then encouraged Emmi to step outside and observe the fist indentations at the back of the vehicle.

"*Oh my God*," she said, reaching up and sliding her hands over the matching metal pits. "Charlie, I'm really glad your…rolling sardine can…was built in a squatch-proof manner."

"That's for sure. I think she's going to need some TLC when we get home."

With one of the RV doors open, Charlie sat on the steps, engaging his laptop and making note of what had happened the night before. It wasn't a set of notes he had anticipated authoring.

Charlie finally finished his dutiful documentation and said goodbye to Emmi and Brutus…again. He brought Betty down out of the rig to cuddle with Emmi's Miniature Pinscher once more.

"We'll see you again sometime, Emmi. Thanks again!" shouted Charlie out the driver's side window as the now slightly dented Motor Myrtle slowly trundled away from Emmi's place toward home.

14

There's No Place Like...

Charlie steered Motor Myrtle back out onto US-64, traveling east this time. Before long the group hit US-550 south/southeast and stayed on that for a little more than an hour. Representing the long road back toward the larger New Mexico cities, the 550 highway makes its way beneath mountaintops and past vast, open plains, Indian reservations, desert National Monuments and stunning rock formation scenery. Myrtle picked up Route NM-96 east near the town of La Jara for another hour of eastward open-space driving, then finally took US-84 east and US-285 south toward Santa Fe.

As Charlie neared his destination on now-familiar roads, his mind spun through the many places he'd seen, people he'd met and creatures he'd tracked on this long journey (not to mention all the local food fare he and Betty had sampled.) All in all, Charlie considered the experience a fairly successful and sometimes astonishing trip. He was glad that he and his pooch had come so far safely, and now he'd get to reconnect with his loving (although oft-zinging) wife, just prior to Thanksgiving.

Charlie pulled up to his own driveway at mid-afternoon after a more than three-hour trek from northwestern New Mexico this day. He wanted to cover the final travel stretch in one uninterrupted driving session if feasible. He'd done it.

As Charlie backed the rig into his driveway, he saw that his home looked unchanged from the time of his departure several months before. He took much comfort in returning to and re-engaging with the sight of his inviting pueblo-style house tucked into the fringes of the desert.

Another of the more gratifying sights Charlie took in upon his return was that there were no apparent clown cars or elephants clogging up the driveway. Thus he could back all the way to the rear of his driveway to stow the rolling rig—without the input of circus stalwarts such as uncouth clowns or persnickety pachyderms.

Francesca jogged happily out of the house as Charlie was finishing up with Motor Myrtle. Her long brown hair flowed behind her as she bounced swiftly across the driveway.

As Charlie exited the vehicle with Betty close behind, Francesca ran up to Charlie and very nearly jumped into his arms, giving him a vigorous hug.

"I never thought you'd make it back from the Land of Oz, you rusty old oil can lug!" she said with glee.

"Although it took some…heart…I wasn't sure we'd make it either, dear," said Charlie to his wife. "The oversized monsters of this world are still well-employed and full of stinky spunk."

Charlie then planted Francesca firmly back down onto the ground.

"And I can see that *you've* been well-employed also—very likely at the trough, the bar and the bakery," she said, stepping back just a bit and observing Charlie's current girth, which had noticeably expanded during the trip. "And your little dog looks a bit more like a big-eared barrel than before," added Francesca. Betty yipped at her once, dismissively.

"Now, now...I'll admit that we generously nourished ourselves," responded Charlie in his own defense, "but mostly because the pursuit of gigantic hairy hominids requires abundant nutritional preparedness. Plus, greasy fast food and cold beer can be a suitable salve for loneliness. I've missed you a *lot*, honey."

"I've missed you too, baby," said Francesca, with more sincerity now. "I'm glad you made it safely across all those miles."

"Well, I've discovered that 'safety' is a relative term," said Charlie. He put his arm around Francesca as they walked toward the house, each carrying in some items from the RV. "It's one thing to be fairly safe in your vehicle wearing sunglasses and a seatbelt; it's another thing to have something throw a tree or a snake or a stump at you, or violently bash in your vehicle."

Francesca had no clue about Charlie's references. "Did all those things happen to you out there?" she asked.

"Well, sort of," he replied. "I clearly have a lot to tell you, my dear damsel," he said affectionately as they wobbled inside together. Betty was right behind them.

A little later on, Charlie was walking past the bar area of his home when some new glassware caught his eye. He was exhilarated to see, upon the bar top, bottles of fairly high-end gold tequila, orange liqueur and a beautiful stack of fresh limes that Francesca had apparently purchased and set out. Charlie very much looked forward to cruising margarita-ville with his life partner at his side.

With no other objectives indicated for the day other than staying out of rolling vehicles, Charlie decided to delay his margarita manufacturing no further. He went behind the bar and grabbed two large margarita glasses with wide bowls—the rims of which he soon salted using a cut lime slice to promote salt adhesion. Soon the icy glasses were brimming with gold tequila, orange liqueur, lemon juice, club soda and a lime garnish. In other words, nectar of the gods.

When Francesca walked into the room and spied the yummy concoctions, she immediately said, "My heavens, I broke into the right house today, didn't I?!"

"You certainly did, young lady. Bottoms up!"

And with that, the couple's celebration of homecoming was underway. Somewhere around mondo margarita number two, the day had become a deeply comfortable glide into near oblivion for the Marlowe pair.

As the margaritas flowed and the beagle of the house enjoyed a big new chew bone on the floor, the husband and wife shared accounts of their experiences during the time Charlie and Betty were away.

Of course, Francesca was very interested in the many twists and turns through which her housemates' trip had taken them during the last four months. Charlie offered a near-chronological summary of the highlights and lowlights of the dozen or so locations where he had conducted investigations. Francesca had to shake her head many times at the precarious predicaments that the man and beagle had gotten themselves into since the summer. She said again that she was very glad they had persevered and made a safe return to the comforts of the arid, high desert.

It was also an opportunity for Francesca to recount highlights and lowlights of her four months of flying solo in New Mexico. She chronicled some work intrigue at the college, some clashes with impertinent staff and students, some perturbing car troubles, and some insect encounters (e.g., the tarantula tumult that she had reported to Charlie back in October). Charlie listened closely to each account and provided compassionate color commentary in response.

Francesca also brought Charlie up to speed on what she had done to pass time during the trip. Not only had she caught up on her reading, but she had apparently dabbled extensively in watching Netflix, Hulu and Amazon Prime streaming programs that Charlie wasn't particularly fond of, such as Game of Scones (a competitive medieval cookie-making show); The Batcher (a serial killer beverage-making competition show); and Blotto Ninja Warriors (a show where sozzled athletes clumsily navigate preposterous obstacle courses, often resulting in hospitalization and/or substance abuse counseling). Charlie had to shake his head at some of these modern excuses for entertainment.

Over a spaghetti dinner that night, Francesca and Charlie continued to catch up on everything from health concerns to how the Albuquerque Isotopes AAA baseball team had done this past season. At present, neither the two Santa Fe residents nor the Duke City baseball team were in tip-top shape, it seemed.

As the couple was cleaning up in the kitchen after dinner, Charlie's cellphone rang. The caller was an old bigfoot-hunting pal of Charlie's, Ken Cryder, who lived in Washington state. Ken reported to Charlie that there had been a rash of recent sightings in Skamania County, and he invited Charlie to come up and conduct some fresh investigations with him.

Charlie was immediately excited at the prospect, then he remembered that he was just a few hours off the road from the *prior* bigfoot excursion. Still on the phone, he said, "Well, Ken, I think I'm going to have to discuss this with my wife. She may not want me running off with the dog so soon again." Charlie looked over at Betty, lying nearby on a couch and generating rhythmic, enthusiastic thumps of approval with her tail.

Francesca made a fairly militant hand gesture indicating, "Cover the phone." Charlie did so.

She said to him with a forceful whisper, "The only way you're getting out of here with that dog again is *if I go with you*. What do you think of that, mister rusty oilcan lug?"

After several speechless seconds, Charlie said to his bigfooting buddy, "Uh, Ken, I think I'm going to need to call you back."

About The Author

DON SHEARER has fun with monsters—not so much in person as in concept. Like Charlie Marlowe, the protagonist in this book, Don has been following bigfoot reports for many years. He's always surprised at the new twists and turns that the reported encounters take, suggesting the amazing physical abilities and elusive adaptations that these outsized creatures exhibit.

Don's prior books in the genre to date include *Bigfoot Bedtime Stories: Tall Tales for All Ages* and *From the Deep Forest*. In addition to writing squatch stories, Don is an award-winning musician and has written comedy in both musical and print formats, plus he does health and wellness-related copywriting. His lovely wife BARBARA somehow puts up with all of it—although she hasn't (yet) won awards for her undeniable indefatigability.

Don and Roxie, i.e., Betty beagle.

Made in the USA
Columbia, SC
09 June 2025